My name is Darcy. I see the extraordinary in the everyday and the wonder in the world around me. Hi So Much and welcome to my second book.

As we sit cuddled up, one on top of the other, bellies full from our chips, Lamb-Beth snoozing on our laps, the air shifts from normal to cold but it doesn't touch us; our dozing heads, our holding hands, our floppy socks. I want to stay here in this moment for ever, like a tiny frozen snowflake. Never growing up. Never going to biggerer school. Never, never, never.

Author and illustrator Laura Dockrill is a graduate of the BRIT School of Performing Arts and has appeared at many festival and literary events across the country, including the Edinburgh Fringe, Camp Bestival, Latitude and the Southbank Centre's Imagine Festival. Named one of the top ten literary talents by *The Times* and one of the top twenty hot faces to watch by *ELLE* magazine, she has performed her work on all of the BBC's radio channels, including Gemma Cairney's Radio 1 show, plus appearances on Huw Murray, Colin Murray and Radio 4's *Woman's Hour*. Laura was the Booktrust Online Writer in Residence for the second-half of 2013 and was named as a Guardian Culture Professionals Network 'Innovator, Visionary, Pioneer' in November 2013.

Laura has been a roving reporter for the Roald Dahl Funny Prize, and is on the advisory panel at the Ministry of Stories. She lives in south London with her bearded husband.

After having her stage invaded by fifty rampaging kids during a reading of her work for adults at Camp Bestival, she decided she really enjoyed the experience and would very much like it to happen again. The Darcy Burdock series was the result! Laura would like to make it clear that any resemblance between herself-as-a-child and Darcy is entirely accurate.

'Everyone's falling for Laura Dockrill' —
VOGUE

Hi So Much

Darcy Burdock

LAURA DOCKRILL

CORGI

DARCY BURDOCK: HI SO MUCH
A CORGI BOOK 978 0 552 56608 7

First published in Great Britain by Corgi Books,
an imprint of Random House Children's Publishers UK
A Random House Group Company

This edition published 2014

1 3 5 7 9 10 8 6 4 2

The Random House Group Limited supports the Forest Stewardship Council® (FSC®), the
leading international forest-certification organisation. Our books carrying the FSC label are
printed on FSC®-certified paper. FSC is the only forest-certification scheme supported by the
leading environmental organisations, including Greenpeace. Our paper procurement policy
can be found at www.randomhouse.co.uk/environment

Typeset in 12.5/19pt Baskerville MT by Falcon Oast Graphic Art Ltd

Corgi Books are published by Random House Children's Publishers UK,
61–63 Uxbridge Road, London W5 5SA

www.**randomhousechildrens**.co.uk
www.**totallyrandombooks**.co.uk
www.**randomhouse**.co.uk

Addresses for companies within The Random House Group Limited can be found at:
www.randomhouse.co.uk/offices.htm

THE RANDOM HOUSE GROUP Limited Reg. No. 954009

A CIP catalogue record for this book is available from the British Library.

Printed and bound in Great Britain by
CPI Group (UK) Ltd, Croydon, CR0 4YY

For the dazzling summer that is Angelo
AND
For my granddad Ken Green, it has
been an absolute wonder getting to know
you better, I really like you. LOADS.
I always wanted a granddad like you
and now I have one. You have always
dedicated your own books to others
and now you have one for you.

Chapter One

Oh, and hi so much. I can't believe I have not even started this book and I am already in trouble.

I am in trouble for the most ridiculous reason of all the reasons that ever existed and what is to blame is one answer and one answer only.

MY
BIG
FAT
MOUTH

This is what happened.

My sister Poppy decided that the name of our

across-the-road neighbour, Cyril, sounded like 'Cereal'. Which it does. That was funny. We were laughing. What was *not* funny, apparently, was us calling Cyril 'Cereal' over and over again, to his very own face, and annoying and winding him up so much that he fell backwards into his house and broke an arm.

Mum is this – L.I.V.I.D.

So this is me – making a card.

What do you draw on the front of somebody's *Get Well* card that you helped make *un-well*? I can only think of drawing Cyril himself with a big plaster cast on, which maybe is naughty but I am *not* a magician

and can in no way tell my brain
what to be thinking.

Erm . . . a catapult?

A basketball?

A kite?

I like a catapult best but I can't
exactly remember how they look, so
I ask Mum.

'Mum, what do catapults look like?'

'Why?' she says. 'You're not making one, are you?
Then it will be us in hospital with you with a sore
eye.' I quite enjoy the fact that Mum thinks that
I am capable of creating a catapult.

'No, I'm drawing one,' I sing.

'For what?'

'Cyril's card.'

Dad cackles, and then Mum gives him the looming
stare of death and he pretends to read the Chinese
takeaway menu. We are having noodles, you see.

'Darcy! Drawing a catapult on the front of
somebody's *Get Well* card who has broken their arm

because of something *you* did is not appropriate!' Her words feel like they get screechier and screechier, but I didn't have a Screech-o-mum-meter on me at the time so I can't be sure exactly.

'Why not?' I say.

'Because you are the reason why he *broke his arm.*'

'Mollie!' Dad tuts. 'Don't say that.' Thank goodness for Dad.

'Sorry, monkey,' Mum says. 'I didn't mean that. I'm sorry, just draw something . . . Look, you're a very good drawer and you have a gorgeous imagination. Draw something . . . happy and positive, like some . . . I don't know? *Ducks?*'

Ducks? Quack. Boring.

Cyril only broked his arm for spaghetti's sake; my caretaker from school broked his back diving into a swimming pool when the water was too shallow, so a broked arm is nothing. So he should be grateful. And we all know the only reason he is staying at the hospital is because he wants cuddles from the nurses and loads of grapes, since Mrs Cyril ranned away with a man on the back of a motorcycle. Probably.

Mum is even more cross at me now because she says I should be feeling sorry for Cyril, not being angry at him, but I can't help it. It's not my fault his mum named him something that sounds so much like something you eat for breakfast or that he is clearly the most clumsiest person in the universe.

After a few moments of scribbly crayon and scrunched-up balls of twisty wasted paper I delegate the job of card makerer to Poppy.

'Me?' she says. 'But you NEVER give me the job of card makerer.' She grins in pleasant, warming surprise, knowing I must be in a real struggle.

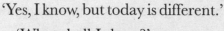

'Yes, I know, but today is different.'

'What shall I draw?'

'Mum says ducks.'

'OK. Cool.' Poppy is a bit too excited for my liking, nudging me out of the chair and squeezing all comfily in herself, fiddling her tiny hands through the colours. So smug.

'Can you even draw ducks?'

'Yeah.'

'Have you actually ever tried?'

'Yes . . .' she lies. I know she is lying because I ALWAYS know.

'When?'

'When I was five.'

'Oh, right.'

It turns out Poppy can't draw ducks. Just as I inspected. Or is it suspected . . . or detected? And then when she realizes that we caused bone-breaking from name-calling, she gets really upset . . .

'We are terrible bullies!' she cries. 'Why us, Darcy? Of all the sisters in the whole entirety of the world, why did somebody get taken to hospital because of something we did?' She flops her head into her hands. I spot she has my glitter love-heart nail varnish on but I don't think this is a time for war.

I quickly remind myself of all the famous scenes I've watched and read about, scenes where girls look after each other. *Little Women*, *A Little Princess*, the ones where they have to live in attics and wear those long gross nighties for bed. I do a bit of acting.

'There, there, hush now, precious one.' The words roll off my tongue effortlessly like I was created for this role. 'We are never alone in this ... harsh ...' – *harsh* was a good word – 'harsh, harsh, cold world, so long as we have each other.' And then I stroke her hair and go in for a good old embrace.

Poppy's tears turned into laughter, a deep wobbly belly roll that first I must say I did take offence to, but it was better than her crying.

'You're stupid.' She smiles.

'Come on then, let's make this card.' And I reach for the most orange bright paper I can find and Poppy sharpens the yellow pencil.

Making art with somebody else is very weird and very strange: it is like being a synchronized swimmer but more

9

harderer because at least they get to practise and plus they get to wear fun swimming costumes. But we are just drawing and painting and scribbling and making and splodging without talking or sharing ideas and just hoping for the best, and I've made a sunflower and carefully painted on each petal by dipping my finger in yellow and printing it round and round in a circle shape. Poppy says I am clever for making petals from fingerprints and I say, 'Don't be silly.' But really I'm thinking, *Thanks*, and also, *Yes, I am*. I say, 'That's amazing, Pops!' about this incredible burst of orange and red dots that she's gone and made and then, 'What is it?'

She replies, 'It's the sunshine, helping make the flower grow more.'

And I feel a bit gulpy and say, 'Let's make the flower and the sunshine touch. So you add the lines of the sunshine ray into my petals and I'll move the fingerprint petals into the sun more.'

'Why, Darcy?' Poppy asks as if I've lost my mind.

'To show they are working together.'

Chapter Two

'Do we *have have have* to?' Poppy is saying as we reach the hospital doors. I don't really *want want want* to but I am curiously excited by the hospital, plus I need a wee.

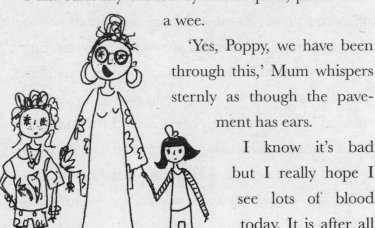

'Yes, Poppy, we have been through this,' Mum whispers sternly as though the pavement has ears.

I know it's bad but I really hope I see lots of blood today. It is after all my last week of holiday before I start *Big really scary big School* and get promoted to being a high mature mighty queen, so I do technically deserve to get to see some blood or at least a rolling eyeball in the corridor.

The doors are automatic and open as soon as our foot gets nearerer. The bushes rattle in applause, it's like they never get over the doors' performance and award a cheer every time.

I can't help thinking about Dad and Hector, at home with Lamb-Beth, all cosied up, probably watching amazing snowy nature programmes about polar bears and penguins and ice. Sometimes I don't like watching these animal nature programmes because often an animal might die from starvation and the camera crew never help the animal. Can't they just take the animals home with them and keep them and be their adopted parents . . . ? A snow leopard would be a siiiiiiicccccckkkk pet. Dad says it's called the 'food chain' but if you ask me it's just plain cold-blooded murder.

The smell of the hospital is all sugary and plasticky

like Play-Doh and our feet squeak on the floor. It is the same sound as we make going around the supermarket but without the possibility of visiting the cake aisle. I know what it also sounds like . . . you know the trainers or 'sneakers' of basketball players when they are 'shooting hoops' on a court? Just like that. (Oh, sorry about me and my b-ball terminology, it's like I get more cleverer by the second.)

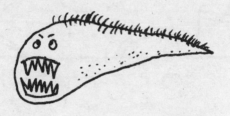

Did you know that lurgies are invisible until they are noticed by somebody with invisibility vision and then they are black slugs with sharp yellow teeth that carry absolutely disgusting diseases like belly aches and snotty noses. So that's why you don't eat anything old or not cooked or bite your nails, and why you must wash your hands when you have been for a wee, and you don't eat crisps after being on the bus, and why you don't hold hands with boys and all that. Hospitals are lurgy dungeons.

RECEPTION

The receptionist teeths us a rotten-lipstick-smothered grin but it looks as though she has been drinking beetroots through a straw for far too long as her lips are all sewn tight together with smudgy purple colour all round them. Perhaps she's a vampire and a hospital is the best place for her to work and she's just come off her lunch break of severed leg?

Mum does all the talking stuff and says we are here to see 'Cyril Flakes'.

Cyril *Flakes*. Cyril *Flakes*? Are you joking me – can his surname really be FLAKES? I never heard of anything so hilarious before but I must not laugh on pain of Mum's looming stare of death. Poppy frowns at me holding my collected smiles in.

'I don't get it,' says Poppy. 'Flakes?'

'Say both names together . . .' I whisper-instruct so Mum doesn't hear and shout at us.

'Cyril Flakes,' she tries, confused.

'No, no, say it like . . . OK . . . say *cereal*.'

'Cereal?' she says. 'But Darcy, we are not allowed to, remember?'

'What, so you think we're never allowed to say the word *cereal* ever again?' I say with sarcasm.

Poppy shakes her head doubtfully. 'I don't think so, no.'

'What do we say then?' I tease her.

'Erm . . . mini . . . biscuit . . . bites . . . with milk?'

I quite like the sound of this actually. Mum gives

us *that* look. She can be a real creaturette. We get a move on.

I know I am not fifteen, but I am certainly extremely *not* a baby. Maybe the nurse was drunk when she took Poppy and me to *this* baby room to wait because it was 'quiet' – apparently we are 'lucky' because there are 'books to read' and 'toys to play with'. *Oh yes,* absolutely plenty of books if we are referring to the bashed-up copy of *Where the Wild Things Are* with the faces ripped out and the squiggly lines all over it that made me want to lose my mind. Or perhaps when she meant 'toys' she was referring to the marvellous raggedy doll with the biro scrawled all over her head? It was just insulting, to be honest.

And I wasn't going to be drinking that overly watered orange squash either. I said, 'I'll have a coffee please,' to the nurse and Poppy gazed at me, like, *WOW, MY BIG SISTER IS A NEARLY WOMAN*. I regretted this immensely, obviously, as coffee is monster poo blended up, and told Poppy I would give her my furry leopard-printy slippers if she let me have four sips of her squash. This was a ridiculous swap, I know that now, but I was desperate.

Cyril cries when he sees us.

Have you ever seen a man cry? It is like watching a car in reverse. You know it can happen but it sort of still looks weird.

'Girls, can you wait outside please?' Mum suggests, but Cyril refuses.

'No, no, please, let them stay . . . *please.*'

We are surprised but quite haps to not be kicked out because being kicked out is horrible, it makes you feel like old flowers or yesterday's newspapers. Poppy hands over our card and I quickly grip the corners too, real fast, to show I made it as well. Cyril does more of that nearly-about-to-cry stuff. Awkward.

'Girls, your card is the most wonderful card I've ever seen.' He looks over it a bajillion times as if his eyes are about to close for ever and he will never get a chance to look at anything again.

I know the card is a stunning bit of work, but perhaps not good enough to receive this praise, but then I remembered: to Cyril, Poppy and I are geniuses. We see ourselves every day so sometimes we don't appreciate that. It makes me sad and happy mixed in together and mostly proud. Mum takes off her glasses and wipes away the steam with her jumper. I can't believe we are not even properly into this book yet and already we are crying. Absolutely X-Zausting! (Do you see what I did there? I used the letter X for 'ex' – if you are feeling cool one day you could try that for yourself. But not in school – school don't like you breaking the rules.)

As we leave Cyril's ward I see a man lying down with a bandage over his eye and he is watching the news with the other one open. I put one hand over my eye to see what it must be like seeing your life through only one eye instead of two. I walk through the corridors with only one eye, peeping around and shyly turning my head to try and get a good look at everything. A girl stares at me with my hand over my eye and makes me feel stupid, so I stop and try and calculate how many footsteps it will take until we are freed from this place.

Ten

Nine

Eight

Seven . . .

That plant needs watering.

Six

Five

Four

Three

Two . . .

Can't believe I didn't even get to see any blood.

Two and a half

One

Out.

In the car I am feeling one bajillion per cent scared about starting school. I don't want *everything to change* or to be any type of fish in any type of pond. *What if I hate my pond? What if I am like Henrietta's fishes in her pond that all ate each other? What then?*

Mum says, 'You OK, monkey?' to me and I nod but I am not, I don't think.

When we get home Dad is watching football and Hector is sleeping with Lamb-Beth curled up. We are starving hungry but Mum says she forgot to get dinner. Good one, Mum. Not.

'It's beans on toast then, kids,' Mum says as she roots through the cupboards. I do love beans so I'm not worried but Poppy hates them so she always has melty cheese instead.

'We could always make THE MIGHTY SAND-WICH!' Dad puts on a Frankenstein voice to say that and Mum giggles. I have never eaten a Mighty Sandwich before but it was clear Mum and Dad had. I couldn't even begin to think what was in it.

'What's in it?' Poppy asks. Good question, Poppy.

'Everything,' Dad says. 'Well, whatever you want. We've got bread, we've got' – he runs over to the fridge and starts rummaging through it, all excited like he's winning a raffle or something – 'butter, cheese, pickle, ham, leftover mash potato, leftover curry.' In a sandwich? 'Pesto, chocolate buttons, yoghurt, gherkins.' Hmmm . . .

THE MIGHTY SANDWICH

Ingredients . . .
You will need:

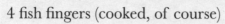
5 slices of bread
   (3 white and 2 brown)
Lots of butter
4 fish fingers (cooked, of course)

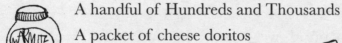
A sprinkle of oven chips (cooked, of course, as well)
1 pot of chocolate mousse
A handful of Hundreds and Thousands

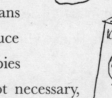
A packet of cheese doritos
A teaspoon of Marmite
A teaspoon of peanut butter
A teaspoon of jam
A spoonful of baked beans
A splodge of tomato sauce
A handful of Rice Crispies

A dash of peanuts (not necessary, but Hector threw them in with the intention of ruining my game plan and I wanted to keep a polka-dot face so I kept them in – they sort of merge with the peanut butter.)
A fried egg with wobbly gooey yellow middle.

Hi, it's me, your favourite chef who isn't allowed to even use an oven. Yes, you've guessed it, Darcy Burdock. Welcome to my cookbook.

First get your five pieces of bread; you can toast them (optional) if you wish or if your bread is a bit stale. Luckily for me, my bread is not that stale so I'm going with not toasting.

Lay the bread out on a chopping board. Make sure the chopping board is not actually a trap door that will make your bread fall through otherwise you will lose sight of your bread for eternity.

Butter the bread.

Stack up ingredients in a tasty order. TIP: place ingredients in an order that makes it appear to others that you are exclusively the only chef in the whole world that could possibly know what order to make this in (but really this doesn't matter).

The best way to enjoy is to start chewing and even if it's not to your taste, still pretend it's gorgeous to the outside world, who will never know otherwise. Which actually is also an excellent tip for life itself.

And I quote . . .

'The best way to enjoy life is to start chewing and even if it's not to your taste, still pretend it's gorgeous to the outside world, who will never know otherwise.'

All right, me making up a saying. I am proud of my own self.

The Mighty Sandwich is absolutely gross. Dad

drives us to the fish and chip shop where we get two massive pillows of family-sized chips drenched in vinegar and salt which was excellent amounts of enjoyable. But Mum ruined the whole experience because she felt guilty that we wasted so much food on our Mighty Sandwiches and so tomorrow we have to take all our books to the charity shop at the end of the road to 'give back'.

I love my mum; everybody knows you can't eat books!

Chapter Three

Later, when I'm sat on the sofa watching television with everyone, I find myself worrying about Big School again and want to tell my brain to behave. When I was younger I wanted a comfort blanket so badly. Did you know, although you may have found this out the hard way, the same rules apply for comfort blankets as they do nicknames . . . you don't get to pick them yourselves. Like a nickname, a comfort blanket must find you.

I was never given a bit of blanket to cuddle or a label to flick or a silkie to stroke or a bobble to gobble – Mum said those kids were annoying, always carrying a dirty old square of material or bit of

T-shirt around with them – but it didn't stop me wanting one. One day when Mum was throwing out the old curtains, I dramatically threw myself onto this one end of curtain, pretending I had a real 'connection' to it and eventually

after much deliberation and annoyance (from Mum's part) she allowed me to rip off a weary bedraggled rag. And this rag soon became my 'comfort blanket'.

Next was the name. All comfort blankets needed a name so that when you referred to them only you and those close knew what you were on about. That's the whole point. It's an attention-seeking thing, a bit like an imaginary friend.

I tried.

Bam-Bam?

No.

Wonky?

Yuck.

Binky? Bong-Bong?

Stupid and babyish.

Huggy?

Too obvious.

And then it hit me. *CUF-CUF*. This was going to be my CUF-CUF.

CUF-CUF would be my only true real actual friend that I would whisper all my secrets into the cottoned ear of. And she would listen and whisper back, probably even she would make me do stuff like insist on eating a series of midnight feasts and snap Poppy's dollies legs off and I'd have to obey, of course. We were bound to have lots of fun together, this comfort blanket and I.

It turned out that CUF-CUF didn't make a very

good friend after all because she didn't do much comforting or whispering and so I got bored of CUF-CUF after a while. It was just one of those things I didn't really need, it turns out. I guess the more olderer you become in life the more your interests change and so do your (big word alert) *priorities*. A priority means the main things you care about more than other things. Like for example, if I sit down to eat a roast dinner my priority is the roast potatoes rather than the broccoli. Well, when I was smaller my priorities were:

Wondering why they hardly ever make trousers for dollies.

Pretending to own a shoe shop.

Pretending to talk on the phone.

Overdosing from a sugar overload.

Lying completely still to convincingly look like I was dead.

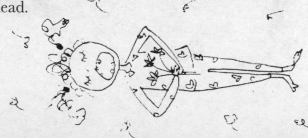

But now my priority is my family.

As we sit all cuddled up, one on top of the other, bellies full from our chips, Lamb-Beth snoozing on our laps, the air shifts from normal to cold but it doesn't touch us; our dozing heads, our holding hands, our floppy socks. I want to stay here in this moment for ever, like a tiny frozen snowflake. Never growing up. Never going to biggerer school. Never, never, never.

Chapter Four

Grandma is staying with us for a bit
– she always does when Dad has
to work away from home.
It's like she and Dad
can't be in the same place
at the same time ... maybe
Grandma is actually Dad dressed
up as a grandma? Oh my goodness! No. That would be stupid
– funny, but mainly stupid.

It is cold today, *ouch* cold.
Summer has been officially
stolen. So cold the air is fizzing

whizzing spinning white particles that are like snow but not as fun or as good because they are not living properly, they are just dissolving like not-ready ice cubes in Coca-Cola. It is 'biting', Grandma says as she wobbles us through the high street, nipping us from shop to shop. Mum's got a cold and is in bed, *cough cough cough.* It is NOT September weather. It's all everybody talks about. The weather is what you're meant to talk about with people that you don't have much in common with; I've been learning this off my grandma. The clouds are fat with rain tears and the pigeons are flapping about all livid and everybody's skin is cracked and scaly like a snake.

We are getting medicine for Mum in the chemist. I'm looking at the packets of hair dye, all those girls

with all that shiny slippery hair, so *brushed*. It flips my belly. I want to dye my hair blue but Grandma won't let me. If I *must* start big school, it would be cool to do it with blue hair. The chemist smells of seashells and mint and, oddly, a bit like smoky bacon.

Back out in the cold again.

Every part of my body is freezing cold for freezing cold's sake, so cold I can't breathe. And the wind is lashing tears out of our eyes that make us all look like we are crying. *Where is the summer?* The sky is a cold concrete grey, moody and marbly and giving away no secrets. The puddles are deep. Each tree stands like the open claw of a frightening creature, naked and charcoaled and worrying me.

Put some clothes on, trees. Keep warm, I am thinking.

It's sprinkling rain but it's too windy to have our umbrellas up so instead we have to get cold and wet and unhappy. Plus Grandma's walking pace is basically this – a slug.

Who on earth does this weather think it is?

When we get back indoors, Grandma shouts, 'Halllllllooooooo!' up the stairs and then slams her hand over her mouth when she remembers Mum must be sleeping. 'Crumbs!' she says as she ushers us in the house, muttering at us to keep quiet, followed by lots of 'oh dear, oh dear' and various other mumbling-under-breath terms.

Dad is away for work with silly John Pincher, like I told you, so the house is major messy because he is the one who does most of the tidying. There are little dots in the carpet from Lamb-Beth's moulting speckled fur fluff . . . technically that is actually my job to clean but it's boring so I don't often get round to that one.

'Get the kettle on, love,' Grandma says to me as she unzips Hector's coat, struggling and complaining about the cold and the chill and the bite and the freeze and how numb her hands are and how she can't feel a thing. I feel sorry and sad when I see the wrinkled skin on her dainty fingers as they work on

Hector's fiddly toggles, and his bright little pink nose is leaking two clear gooey lines of snot. Like space jelly. Uck.

Hmmmmmm. Hmmmmmm. Hmmmmmm. I'm thinking as I'm waiting for the kettle to boil. I've been allowed to make tea for only a couple of months now and Grandma is seriously taking advantage of this – she uses language to make it seem like making tea is easy, like:

'TIP me out a tea, would you, dear?'

Or:

'POP the kettle on, would you, love?'

Or:

'NIP in the kitchen and POUR us out a cuppa.'

These words such as TIP and POP and NIP and POUR do not demonstrate the actual physical and technical skill involved in making a cup of tea.

Hmmmmm.

Poppy is still not allowed to make tea because of the hot water in case she burns herself. A friend of a friend of a friend that I know has no belly any more because of burning herself with hot water. She actually has a big space in the middle of her body, so you do have to be *so* careful.

I get two teaspoons and pretend I am in a band whilst I'm waiting for the kettle to boil. I drum the spoons on the sugar pot, the coffee pot, the tea bag pot and the milk. The kettle noise is the bass.

'Aw, you, my Darcy, should win the best granddaughter in the world

award,' Grandma cheers as I careful-gently carry her teacup in its tinkering saucer.

They *should* start a 'Best Granddaughter in the World Award' – I could have a decent shot at winning that. I *am* pretty good.

I sit down next to her and rest my head on her shoulder. I think about sneaking upstairs and seeing Mum but Grandma says she is sleeping.

Then a little white envelope plops through the letter box with 'Darcy and Poppy' written on the front in shaky ugly hand lettering. *Mysterious*, I think, and shout Poppy's name, before getting told off by Grandma for making too much noise.

We nestle down on the sofa, fighting over the corners, and together, sort-of-ish, rip open the envelope and two packets of sunflower seeds fall out all over our laps with a little card:

Thank you for my card with the sunflower on the front, here are some seeds to plant some sunflowers of your own.

From Cyril,
your next door neighbour.

We both look towards the window: on the pavement outside, a woman's umbrella folds itself inside out in a gust of wind and Poppy looks as though she is about to cry. I don't think I would like

38

to be born in this weather if I was a sunflower. I put the seeds on the side and decide we should wait for that fashionably late sun to show its stupid face. If it ever will again.

Chapter Five

They were big. They were ugly. They were wretched
and horrid and reminded me mostly of every single
worst thing in the world.

My new school shoes.

I HATE them, I am thinking,
but can I say this? *NO.*

WHY not? *Because Grandma
chose them.*

'What about the clogs?' I cry.

'They didn't have any backs to them.' Grandma
reaches for her purse.

'The . . . trainers?' I try desperately.

'Don't be silly.'

'The panda-bear sandals?'

'They are for infants.'

'The high-heel ones?'

'Don't be so *repulsive*.'

They CAN'T be my shoes. They can't be *anybody's* shoes! They clearly are a factory malfunction major mistake that somebody got fired for. Or a prank. My eyes fill with water as we leave the shop, the woman waving us out and probably shaking her head thinking to herself, *What a pair of idiots*, knowing that nobody would ever buy themselves such ghastly footwear. Then again, what else should I have expected, letting an ancient antique come shoe-shopping with me? It's my own entire miserable fault.

Poppy thinks the whole thing is

H-I-L-A-R-I-O-U-S.

And my depression has given her some kind of new energy, which is managing to make her skip crazily down the street in absolute smug joy. I think about throwing one of the shoes heftily at her back but am frightened that the shoe is *that* heavy it could quite possibly kill her. So I resist.

'They are very practical.' Grandma smirks delightfully proudly over our *stop-off for tea*, and Poppy laughs her head off.

'Yeah, practical for running away from all the bullies,' she says. She does actually have a point.

The shoebox sits under my bed like a coffin. It

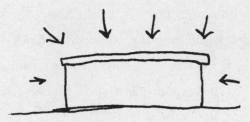

matches the prison garments that I am expected to wear with them. How on earth am I meant to show off my dazzling personality in all that gross *grey*? When I got 'accepted' at the school I clearly recall Mum saying, 'You will love the uniform.' And I remember thinking, *Unless it is the same uniform amazing people get to wear when they are doing nothing except having fun and not being scared, then I don't want to wear it.* But I don't have One. Single.

Choice. It is hideous. Grey and like sewage. I can't bear it.

'Let's see you then, monkey.' Mum's eyes peel open wide, making all this going-to-Big-School thing a massive chunky deal.

'I hate the uniform, Mum,' I growl.

'I can't do anything about that, love, plus once you're there you'll forget all about it because everybody will be wearing the same thing.'

'Well, you *could* do something about these shoes, surely?' I kick one of the shoes into the wall.

'Don't do that, Darcy, you'll scuff them!' Mum squeaks. 'And look at the wall.' She tuts and licks her thumb and rubs the wall like a lizard but it makes the mark a bit bigger. She breathes through her nose which means she's 'on the brink' (basically going mad).

'Good. I want to scuff them. Not the wall. These shoes,' I moan to get back onto the shoe topic. 'They are ugly and big and all . . . dompy.'

Mum laughs. 'What did you call them?'

'Dompy.'

She likes it. She laughs. 'Dompy. I see what you mean. They are sort of . . . dompy.'

'See?' I begin to laugh too.

'Why don't you write a story about these . . . dompies? You never know, it might convince you to like them . . . just a little?'

'I doubt it.'

I line the shoes up on the kitchen table and stare at their brown leather and ugly buckle. I flick open my writing book and begin . . .

Have you ever heard of a new and tiresome beast called 'the Dompy'? No?

Of course you have not, Over-Keen One, because I just made it up.

Well, this beast is the most ridiculous creature ever. They look like a large shoe. They are brown. They have skin like an elephant. They have a beak like a platypus, eyes like beetles and a mouth like an upturned horse hoof. Their ears are tiny. The species of Dompy is very almost impossible amounts of rare. The Dompy is a lonely and feeling-sorry-for-itself type of creature, who finds being alive quite tough. The most recognizable and unique feature of the Dompy is its oversized hunchback that is full of Dompy worries. The Dompy's worries are really full of silly made-up things that aren't even true — like 'everybody hates me because of my ugly hunchback' — but all that happens by the Dompy worrying about his ugly hunchback is that the hunchback just gets bigger, then the Dompy will start to worry about the hunch getting bigger which then just only goes on to make the hunch even bigger and then he worries about that, which then makes the hunch on his back bigger and makes him sadder and lonelier and grumpier and all the while the hunch grows and his confidence shrinks.

The Dompy felt so fed up. Sometimes he would stare at his lonesome reflection in the lake and let the ripples of the water surface take his hunchback away for a second, but it never worked, it was just an illusion. He would look on at the other spring-footed, light-speed-whipping mammals parading around, frolicking and rolling and hopping and jumping, and then back at his reflection and he would think, Why me? and the hunch would grow another bunch.

'There's nothing wrong with you, mate,' Toad ribbitted. 'Look at my chin, it goes on for miles, look at my warts, they're horrible things but it's what makes me who I am.'

'Easy for you to say, you've got plenty of friends who love you for who you are,' the Dompy grunted sulkily.

'Well, maybe if you stopped whining and whingeing so much, you'd have more friends,' Toad snubbed.

'Well, maybe if I had MORE friends, I wouldn't NEED to whine and whinge!' the Dompy protested.

Then out of the reeds came the charcoal-coloured Bully Cat. He was big and gruff and sniffed and

snuffed and spat but was the most respected
and powerful beast on the planet. He had come
to sip from the lake.

'Good afternoon, Bully Cat,' Toad croaked,
tidying around his little corner of lily pad as
though Bully Cat had entered his home to
inspect it.

'Good afternoon, Toad,' Bully Cat purred.

Toad nodded to the Dompy, signalling him
to greet Bully Cat, and as nervous as he was
after his little pep talk with Toad, the Dompy
did as he was advised.

'Good afternoon, Bully Cat.'

And Bully Cat finished drinking from the
lake, sniffed, snuffed, swallowed and spat and
slid away from the lake,
ignoring the Dompy
completely and
the Dompy's
hunch grew
a bunch.

'Oh no — my hunch, look it's even bigger
— what did I do wrong, Toad? I don't
understand.' The Dompy wanted to cry.

'Me neither,' Toad sympathized, 'but let's not
give up yet, we can always say good afternoon
to somebody else and see if they will be your
friend.'

'I don't think I can take any more rejection
today,' the Dompy cried.

'Don't be silly,' Toad reassured. 'Bully Cat is
difficult to impress . . . look, there's Panda Paw,
he's friends with everybody, he will certainly
say good afternoon and want to make friends
with you.'

'Do you think so?' The Dompy looked at his
feet. 'I do like the sound of being mates with
Panda Paw.'

Toad hopped over to Panda Paw who was
sleepily lazing under a tree.

'Good afternoon, Panda Paw! Wakey wakey!'
Toad croaked.

'Ah, good afternoon, Toad, lovely to see you.' Panda Paw yawned a great yawn and stretched.

Toad winked at the Dompy, who did as he was told and managed to gurgle out, 'Good afternoon, Panda Paw!' before waiting for the warm reply. But instead he just heard snores coming from Panda Paw's nostrils. 'He didn't even notice me!' the Dompy cried as his hunch grew a bunch.

'Maybe he didn't see you?' Toad suggested, which he knew was stupid as Toad was about the same size as the Dompy's ankle. 'OK, maybe he did, he was probably just tired. Look, let's find somebody else to say good afternoon to instead, somebody who isn't Bully Cat or Panda Paw.'

'I don't think I can take any more hurt today.' The Dompy kicked the grit on the floor below and it hit him back in the face. 'I'm so useless and rubbish and ugly, it's not a surprise nobody wants to be my friend.'

'Don't say that, cheer up. Look, there's Parrot — she's a flirt, she likes everybody, she will say good afternoon.'

The Dompy didn't seem hopeful but it wasn't like his day could get any worse.

Parrot was in the coconut tree, combing her rainbow feathers and humming a love song.

'Good afternoon, Parrot,' greeted Toad, 'you look nice today.'

'Toad, you gentleman, it's so lovely to see such a handsome face on such a beautiful day!' she sang and carried on combing her feathers, trying to look as pretty as possible. The Dompy was so nervous; his big legs went all fizzy and liquidy like they were full of lemonade. Toad cocked his head at him.

'Good afternoon, Parrot, you look like a vision of summer,' the Dompy managed to squeeze out, before blushing a violent violet and turning away, trembling, waiting for it all to be over. Toad seemed impressed but the Dompy wasn't so sure — maybe the summer line was too forward, too keen? He was embarrassed of himself.

Parrot said nothing and continued grooming herself. The Dompy's hunch grew another bunch.

'Very weird,' Toad said as they walked away.

'Oh well,' the Dompy sulked. 'Thank you for trying.'

'I'm sorry, Dompy, it seems nobody hears you. I did try to help you.' And Toad hung his head low too: he felt like he had failed the Dompy.

And then they heard Parrot say, 'Good afternoon, Parrot, you look like a vision of summer.' She was repeating it, over and over again.

Toad hopped back to the coconut tree. 'So you did hear him?' He leaped with happiness over to Parrot.

'Hear who?' Parrot chirped.

'The Dompy, you heard him say good afternoon to you. You must have because you're a parrot and you repeat what you hear!'

'Oh, I must have done, but I don't remember seeing him!' Parrot held a wing over her eyes to block the sunshine out so she could have a good look.

'You know him, he's kind and gentle and sweet and silly, you must know the Dompy.' Toad looked around. He could see the Dompy all right, in the shade trying to seem invisible. Toad beckoned him forward. 'She heard you, Parrot heard you, come on . . .'

And the Dompy stepped forward into the light, his sad eyes wary.

Parrot looked him up and down and then clapped her wings in delight. 'Ah yes, there he is, the Dompy, and he's your friend, is he, Toad?'

'Yes, I suppose he is.' Toad smiled, and then said proudly: 'He definitely is.'

'Well, any friend of yours, Toad, is a friend of mine.' Parrot screeched, 'Hellllllllllloooooooo, Dompy, what cute little ears you've got.' She giggled and the Dompy blushed and said hello back. His hunchback shrank – he couldn't believe it.

'Toad has been a very good friend to me,' the Dompy laughed. 'He has made me happier

with myself, he makes me feel good.' The words
tumbled out and they felt alien to him, he had
never said anything so positive before. His hunch
shrank some more.

'We should throw a party in the Dompy's
honour! Let's invite Panda Paw and Bully Cat
and all the others. I want them all to meet the
Dompy, I know they will love him just as much
as us!' said Dompy's new friend Toad, and
Parrot agreed in delight.

Panda Paw and Bully Cat came to the
coconut tree with lots of others, where they ate
warm golden sponge cake with rose-petal crystals
on top, satsuma-ade, palm sugar and maple
syrup pie, cauliflower and strawberry cookies
and tomato heart tarts and plenty of home-
made honey beer. The Dompy was known for
a sweet tooth, and as his belly got fatter, his
hunch got smaller and the more friends he made.

The moral to the story — if you don't love and

respect yourself, how will anybody else learn to
love and respect you either? The same applies
to shoes.

I try the Dompy shoes on again. I *still* hate them,
but it looks like I'm going to have to start accepting
them if I want others to accept me too.

Chapter Six

The time has come. The one I putted to the back
of my mind for approximately one billion years: the
night before BIG School. Duh. I know you don't call
it that in *real* life, I know it's fine to call it secondary
school, or even *work* if you feel like it. But that doesn't
change the fact that it is big, very big, and that means
one giant big scary headache that makes me as tiny
as the rainbow-coloured paracetamol trying to
conquer it.

For my last supper Mum is making chilli; she
is using a garlic crusher. The garlic goes in whole
and comes out in smushed-up bits. It's good. I think
it's my favourite kitchen appliance. I think about

staining the wretched uniform in the chilli or at least with the garlic and then not having to wear it; although luckily I think before I act and realize this will most likely end badly for me.

Dad comes home with swooping arms and love, picking me up and cuddling me and letting me tug his beard, but no intense amount of tugging is going to drag me out of this worry well.

All that night, my throat is like glue and my new school is like a tall shadow that I tried to ignore for so long, but it's there all grey and brown like an abandoned factory. I have seen the big kids coming out of there too; linking arms and wearing high shoes and saying swear words even if they want. And then I push it all to the back of my head like a feeling I don't want to deal with.

How am I ever going to fit in? I think.

'You just need to walk in that place with your head held high,' Dad says.

BUT I CAN'T!

There is so much to think about, so many things:

what about the class plant Tina who lives at my old school? Who will water her now without me keeping a watchful eye? Who will know that the tap in the girls' toilet gets really hot and you have to fill the sink one part cold to three parts hot to properly wash your hands? And that the hopscotch mat is missing the letter 3 in the playground outside so you have to improvise? Who will ring the bell at lunch time to let everybody know it's time to eat? Aarggggggghhhhh! My old school will not possibly cope without me.

How will all the new stuff at this new school possibly squeeze into my head . . . *what if I pop?* What if all my ideas add up so much they just edge nicely out of any open hole they can? My nose? My eyeballs? My ears? I look over the mile-long list of things I need to bring with me. Stupid things that I never imagined even owning myself, like AN ACTUAL *personal* calculator, indoor *and* outdoor trainers, and textbooks. My rucksack looks even more biggerer than when I run away from home,

it's like I'm leaving for ever.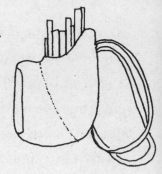
Darcy on a train to Big School,
never to return again.

On the first day of the end
of my life (school) it wouldn't be
too much to ask to expect a boily
egg and soldiers, would it? Pah! But obviously Mum
has had her head in the clouds because I'm having
to eat a breakfast of muesli (hamster bedding) that
gets swallowed in huge lumps that don't settle in my
tummy in no way whatsoever. I cut my gum whilst I
brushed my teeth and keep looking at myself in the
mirror a trillion times and not feeling one bit like me.
I feel like a fraud. Like an actor. I feel small and old
at the same time. Like an . . . ancient Chihuahua.

I want to cry the whole way there and even when
Mum wants to take photographs of me I am feeling
stupid about my frilly socks and insecurely want to
fold the frills into the socks themselves so nobody
can see. The sleeves of my jacket are *too* long – I
could possibly never have arms like this – and the

skirt is *even* longer, like a proper hippy length. The only way I am going to get through these school years is to pretend the uniform is more colourful. A nice purple blazer instead of this wretched thing, and maybe even stripey socks. But no amount of make-believe is going to make these Dompies anything other than ... well, pretty ... dompy. Leaving my house I wonder will I ever see it again? Will I make it through the day? I go to close the front door and that's when I see Lamb-Beth sitting outside on the step with her 'going to the park lead' in her mouth.

'No, Lamb-Beth, you can't come. I'm sorry.' I pick her up and breathe in her fluff and ripple her ear in between my fingers and we snuggle. I wish I could spend the day with her. I let her back into the house but she keeps wanting to come out again. That's the trouble with the six-week holidays: you almost forget you have to do anything with your life ever again, and she's got too used to having me around.

We drive past my old school on the way to my new one. Poppy and Hector get out of the car, running towards the tiny familiar gate. I draw an invisible star on the car window with my finger and say goodbye. When we reach the driveway of my *new* school I am met by absolute ridiculous madness. Everybody seems so growed up, it's like walking into a nightclub. Nobody has these long sleeves or hippy long skirts or dompy bench shoes that I have. Nobody has frilly socks on either, or rucksacks like they are leaving the country. Everybody seems to know each other.

I try to look as though I am not looking for Will, or Caroline from the Magical Land of China, who is also coming to this school. I'd even like to see hateful Clementine, as at least she is familiar. It feels like that bit in the penguin nature programme when all the mum penguins come home from food catching and come to meet their husbands and eggs and it's complete major chaos. It's all beaks and wings.

'Hiya, Darcy, and everything.'

Will. Thank goodness. I look at him in his uniform. It's *way* too big, his sleeves are nearly brushing the pavement and he's gone for a new hairstyle.

'Is that gel in your hair?' I ask. He goes to pat it and then remembers he must not want it to be one bit ruined.

'I'm not sure, Annie did it.' Annie is Will's big sister who has already even finished big school and knows about everything cool so I nod in approval.

'It looks nice.'

'Thanks.'

Will is the most frightened I have ever seen him. I want to hold his hand but I just don't know if this is allowed at Big School.

The building is even greyer and more boring when we get closer up.

The kids are even biggerer and the feeling is even scarier. You can recognize all the new ones like us from miles away. We are all the ones that are too small, waiting to get stepped on like ants.

'What if people *hate* us?' Will suddenly says to me. He's not allowed to do this fear business, he is supposed to be the brave one, the one that knows what's going on . . . but he does have a point. What *if* people hate us? What will we do then? How will we make sure we look cool? What if we get tied up to the front gates and get force-fed dog poo and nits? What if we get stapled to the notice board? What if we . . . get made *deaded*?
What then, *eh*?

I grab Will firmly by
the wrist and bring him
round to face
me. He panics
and flinches as if I am
about to either snog
him or punch him, but
I don't do either as obviously I am not a maniac.

'William Hopper, we *can* do this because when it comes to being a human being we are the very best, we are *superheroes* at being human beings and nothing is going to bring us down or ruin our chances at making this school work for us because . . . well, because this school needs *us* far more than we need it. In fact, this school is begging for cool kids like us to come and electrify its corridors and classrooms, so what you saying, bruv? Get your bag on your back, straighten that tie, do up your flies and come on!'

I really was fired up and I feel so strong and powerful and relieved and brilliant, exactly like if I was a Prime Minister-ess for my actual paid job. There is a moment's silence and that is when everybody begins to laugh, hard. I've not only given this speech to Will, I've given it to the whole playground. I melt. I am a puddle.

Will reaches round in the awkwardness and slowly does up his flies; the zipping sound pierces the air like a horn on a clown's bicycle whilst the dreaded one and only Clementine claps her hands slowly in mocking meanness. What a wicked way to start secondary school, I think. *Well done, Darcy, well done.*

Chapter Seven

Will and I have been putted on different sides of the room to force us to make 'new' friends. I knew we should have lied and said that Will was Australian – we could have made a whole storyline up that he was raised in the Outback by hunters and has only just moved over here to start school. Then we could have pretended we never met before and could actually secretly stick together. But great: too late.

I am sitting next to a girl called Sasha whose nose is constantly running into her lip and that is a no-go for Big School. I am also sitting next to a boy with an amazing afro but every time his head turns to the side

his hair brushes past my face. UUUUGGGGGHHH!
Annoying! But at least Will's in my class.

Of all the teachers I've seen walking
around this ghastly factory building,
trust us to get Mrs Ixy. Her hair is
black and long and tangly and her
skin is pale and her voice is croaky
and her ideas are all annoying and
weird, like, 'Let's play a name game' and I
know she only wants to play a 'name game'
so that she can learn our names to ensure
she gets them correct on the menu when
she serves us up at a feast for witches.

She starts by handing us out lined paper, which she serves up like bad news with long spiky nails, flicking her eyes at us, which are dark and demonic and scary. I am so livid I never sawed this before. *Of course* a teacher could be a witch, it is the best chance to get as close up and personal to a child as you could possibly be to ensure perfect snatching distance.

This annoying girl called Bella takes a little comb out of her pencil case and without ASKING me begins brushing my hair. I don't want to be rude so I don't do anything. Then Mrs Ixy says she wants 'Complete silence' but obviously didn't hear the scrapes and scratches of my hair being detangled. It is really a bit pulling and then Bella begins separating my hair to probably do bunches and I just turn round and say, 'Stop it!' and she doesn't stop so I push her hand off mine and she says, 'OUCH! You didn't need to HIT me!' really loud, and Mrs Ixy looks up and says, 'Who's hitting who?'

And Bella says, 'SHE' – meaning me – 'hit me.' She says it a bit shyly because she knows it was provoked. She isn't a bully girl or anything, just a wanting-to-work-in-a-hairdresser's type who wants to practise.

Mrs Ixy says, 'Is this true, Darcy?'

And I say, 'No, she was playing with my hair.'

Some people in the class do that horrible laugh like a sneeze and Mrs Ixy says, 'I didn't ask *why* you hit her, I asked you *if* you hit her.' And I have no choice but to nod. Mrs Ixy addresses us all like this: 'You are Year Sevens now, this is NOT primary school, there will be NO excuses for CHILDISH behaviour.' And then moves on to our writing exercise.

Will looks down at his page pretending not to know me a bit and Bella whispers 'Sorry' in my ear and I feel so embarrassed and like I take up all the space in the classroom. I want to go home already. I HATE Mrs Ixy.

We have to write on the page 'about ourselves'. We have to say who we are, our age, who we live with, what we like . . . Well, I do not trust this sheet of evidence one bit. I mouth-sign-whisper to Will, 'Do NOT fill this in,' and point at the sheet, but he is on the other side of the room and cannot hear and mouths back 'WHAT?' and so I point back at the sheet and then shake my hands over it and then he shakes his head and looks at Mrs Ixy. *Whatever*, Will, suit yourself, you will be sorry when you get stolen and turned into stew.

ABOUT ME

My name is Caterpillar Louise Porridge and I am 22, so really old to be honest and I wouldn't taste yummy at all if anybody ever

wanted to eat me, I am very out of date.
I came to school because living in the jungle
was just too hot and I had outgrown all
the animals and tropical exotic plants with my
wisdom and excellence and also I wanted to
get betterer at adding and dividing. I don't
really need to be here because I am really
already clever at everything. I am a black belt
in karate. I once sawed a man's head off with
my armpit and can speak every language that
exists, even alien. I know all the words to every
film and song. I am also doubling up as a spy
and television reporter. My favourite colour is
blood. I have bodyguards hidden in nooks and
crannies at all times so there is not one point
in trying to steal me because you will instantly
be gobbled up by my 1000 rattlesnakes and
bears or, if you are lucky, put into a boring
prison with nothing fun to do, not even drawing.
My mum is a millionaire Oscar award-winning
actress but you've never heard of her because

only selected viewers who are mostly the winning members of society can watch her films and my dad lives in a Greek Myth, inventing a way of bringing unicorns over here to England. In my spare time I rehearse new kung fu moves and create odourless poisons. If I like I can hop in my private jet and visit my cowboy relatives in Montana. As I say I am just here to revise and further my interest in sums and then I will be nothing but dust on your desk . . . I am immortal . . . which means I will never be dying so don't even try . . . or else.

P.S. I do not know who Darcy Burdock is, and in fact am sure she does not exist.

P.P.S. I have got a garlic crusher that is made actually for you to put your nose in and get broken and force-fed the eternal smell of garlic, and I carry that with me at all hours.

Well, if that doesn't do the trick then I'll be damned (I don't know what this means but I heard it said in a film).

The bell rings for lunch. Will and I stick to the walls like we are spineless whilst the rumbling avalanche of bigger students rushes through us, tearing little ones off the staircase, picking them off like flower heads, barging shoulders and elbowing. Luckily too much is going on for him to remind me about already getting told off by Mrs Ixy, so we just follow the protesting stampede to the dinner hall, which smells of oven. Lunch time is not like how I imagined. There isn't a jukebox for starters like how the American TV shows promised I'd have at Big School. Also there wasn't anybody dancing on tables or doing rap battles in little huddles. There were no gangs of goths or punks or rude girls. Nobody carry-hugs their books to their chest and slams their lockers like on TV too. Nobody has an apple. All I can see is the same grey uniform repeating over and over and over and over again, and queues of people holding trays and moving so fast, exactly knowing what they wanted to order before they'd even looked at anything. Even though Will and I have packed lunches I have a quick sneak peek and am amazed to see rows of hot sugary doughnuts, swelling muffins, pots of wedges and trays of noodles, piles of chips, sausages, fish fingers, toasties . . . *burgers with buns*? Mac'n'cheese! Nobody is eating boring things like a *sandwich*. I am fed up and look at my mushy banana. Will looks at his tinfoil box of limp treasure.

'Wish we were having burgers,' he says.

'Why can't we?' I ask, though my tummy basically says this for me in rumbles.

'We don't have any money.'

'Money? You don't need to bring *money* to school, you *idiot*.'

'You do need it, look.' Then to my absolute mighty horror, Will points to a tall wiry goggle-glasses woman in a little white paper hat typing numbers into a till and giving students their change. Will was *right*. This was like McDonald's. Or somewhere else just as fancy that people who work go to in their lunch hour. This was  like being catapulted into being a growed-up human adult in one second.

Will murmurs, 'I wish I had money.'

And I whisper back, 'Me too.'

How confusing, in our old school *nobody* wanted school dinner and now here everybody couldn't get enough of it. We thought we were the clever ones bringing our own stuff in, but we weren't. Not at all. Resigned to our lunch boxes I huff and try to

look cool but there isn't an *obvious* place to sit or *be*, and every time you go to sit somewhere, somebody rushes in before you've even blinked. Now I know why Mum gets so stressed in the Tesco car park. Will and I hardly say a word to each other, chewing and swallowing, just waiting for the day to roll to a close.

This school day seems like a lifetime and I am nearly falling asleep in my chair when 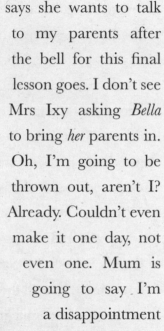 Mrs Ixy calls me over and says she wants to talk to my parents after the bell for this final lesson goes. I don't see Mrs Ixy asking *Bella* to bring *her* parents in. Oh, I'm going to be thrown out, aren't I? Already. Couldn't even make it one day, not even one. Mum is going to say I'm a disappointment and I'm going to have to be homeschooled by Grandma and learn only about old things whilst Will goes on to be an excellent magician or something.

Feel sick.

Dad is waiting in the car to collect me. It is embarrassing because he has taken the afternoon off to pick me up and has hip-hop music blaring and sunglasses on to look cool but it's so *disturbing*. I wish I was small again and could wrap up in clingfilm like a small soggy soft sandwich in a Barbie lunch-box. He is waving energetically but still kind of trying to have a *keeping it casual* sort of look about him. I am so worried that I must ruin his efforts with my bad news that I've only been at school for roughly approximately 0.4 seconds and my teacher has already requested to see my dad.

'There's my big monkey!' He is so happy. 'Check out my *swag*!' He slaps the steering wheel. 'Let's go and get a milkshake! Strawberry for the lady!'

He winks . . . and then I cry. I am sad because this is not how I had imagined this day to go. I wanted us to have a milkshake and talk about how cool and inspiring my new teacher is and all the new friends I made and all the new amazing things I learned, like how heavy the planets are and what giraffes eat and how long it takes for a light bulb to come on and what another word for 'vomit' is and what 51,237 plus 89,762 is and if vampires exist and what all the types of butterfly are, but I don't know any of this. All I know is Dad has to see the teacher. Then he takes his sunglasses off.

'Oh, no, Darcy, what's the matter? Don't cry. I'm sorry, I was playing, I was being silly. I am sorry.'

'It's not that,' I sniffle.

'Well, what is it then?' He is really worried and that makes me sadderer.

'It's my new witch teacher, she wants to speak to you.'

'What? She wants to talk now?'

I nod. I see a tear fall onto my new blazer, worming its cheeky way into the yuck material.

Dad gets out and locks the car, he checks himself in the mirror – *see*, even *he* is terrified of this school business.

'Come on then, monkey. Dad's here.'

I lead Dad into my classroom, where Mrs Ixy is sitting filing some work away into beaten up cabinets.

'Mr Burdock? Hi, I'm Mrs Ixy, you can call me Barbra.'

Barbra. Barbra is NOT a witch's name.

'Hi, Barbra, I'm Darcy's dad and personal *idiot*.' He giggles, trying to make a joke, but Mrs Barbra Ixy is not amused. Dad looks embarrassed.

'Thanks for popping in.'

'Not at all.'

'I want to talk to you about Darcy.'

'Phew, glad it's not about me!' Dad jests, but no, it doesn't work.

I am shaking. I have never felt this frightened because it feels like an axe is about to fall on me at any moment and take my life away. I am going to get kicked out. I am going to never get a job in real life or be able to drive a car like Will's big sister Annie or go shopping in expensive shops. I'll have to leave my house and become a person that has to forage for fruits and berries and live in a cardboard house. Or worse, go back to my original future ambitious career plan . . . being a grandad.

'Mr Burdock, your daughter Darcy has a stunning imagination.'

I've heard this one before . . . and so has Dad by the looks of things.

'Really, Mr Burdock, I think Darcy is very talented, her writing today was easily the best in class – perhaps the best I've seen at this age.'

My dad's face pours open into sunshine and so does mine.

'Wow, that's come as a surprise, I mean, not a surprise, I knew she was talented, she's always writing, she's writing all the time, I mean, she's writing every day, about everything, she never stops, she can go for hours, you should see her writing books, no you should read the one about the Octopus – what's it called, love?'

'The Octopus story?' I say, all proud and tangled up in a mixed emotion bag, and Mrs Ixy is smiling widely.

'Yeah. It's really, really good.' Dad has got carried away and is a bit out of breath.

'Her last school sent me some of her creative writing and she did lots in class today. I would like

Darcy to write for the school magazine, Mr Burdock – what do you think about that, Darcy?'

'OK,' I say, because I can't think of any other words. My brain has vanished on to catch the next train of thought where I can see myself with a ginormous quill on a posh writing desk dressed in some beautiful quilted two-piece power suit, scribing paragraphs of excellence for the rest of my life and never getting in trouble. They might even use my face on the £5 note one of these days. THAT is how excellent I am.

Chapter Eight

At home, Mum smiles broadly as she begins to pop
peas out of their shells, the soft sound of them tapping
each other gently. She's being all hippy these days
after what she calls 'over-consumption', and drinking
herbal tea and meditating and recycling and fresh
food munching but with the exception of oven chips
and wine because they are her *fix*. A fix is something
that fixes you a small bit when you're down – mine is
chocolate and writing, obviously. (P.S. And biting off
my fingernails occasionally and spitting out the nail
and letting it flllllllllllllllllllllllllllllyyyyyyyyyyyyyyyyyyy
across the room like a skeleton helicopteretta to a
landing which is unknown to the pilot.)

I smile back and check out my milk moustache in the toaster, *looking good*.

'I am so proud, Darcy. Such a hit, and on your first day too! You must be so happy.'

'I am. I have to go to this *meeting* tomorrow first thing, with all the other magazine people, and decide what I am going to write about. I think I might wear my hair in a professional plait.'

'Good idea. Well, we better give that hair a wash and a brush.'

OH. RIGHT.

And it is a couple of hours later and this is happening . . .

'AAAAAAHHH!'

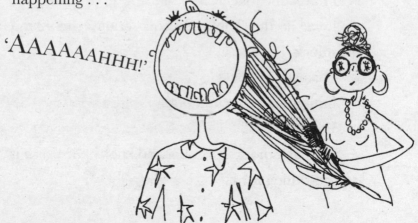

'AAAAAAAAAAHHHHHHGGGGGGGGG!'
I scream.

'Sit still,' Mum says through gritted teeth.

'AAAAAAAAAAHHHHHHHGGGGGGGG!
It kills.'

'Don't be a baby.'

'How am I being a baby? You would never ever in
a zillion years cause this much hell to a baby and also
babies don't have hair like this!'

'Darcy, do you want your hair in a professional
plait?'

'Yes.'

'Well, sit still then.'

'I have a headache.'

'Look at this knot, are you serious? It's like a
dreadlock. Look at it.'

'I want dreadlocks.'

'I might have to cut it out.'

'What?'

'This dreadlock, it's so big and knotty, the brush is
doing nothing for it.'

'It hurts.'

'Darcy, there is the end of a crayon in here.'

'What?'

'Look.' Mum leans her open palm before me and inside the small curve of her hand is the head of a bright pink crayon. 'Ridiculous.'

'I wanted it there,' I say smugly, but really I am thinking, *How on earth did the end of a crayon get in my hair?* My head and eyes and hands feel all fizzy and twinkly from all the stingy vicious clawing of my scalp.

Poppy walks in. *Great.* Her eyes can't help but show me they are happy to see me sweaty and in pain.

'That's why I keep *my* hair straight and short,' she hisses and does a pirouette ballerina-type move that makes me hope she breaks her ankles. 'Always brushed and washed,' she adds and then she gets ready for the big bomb: 'Just how Mum likes it. Always tidy.'

'Always ugly,' I bark back.

'Well, yours always looks like a hairy mammoth,' she snaps.

'Girls. Come on.' Mum's getting irritated, but in a smiley way, one of my favourite ways of how she gets actually, sort of not wanting to laugh but not being able to help it.

The next morning I wake up more professional than even probably a professor. This is how my plait looks – *excellent*.

I stroll quite confidently into school but then I see Clementine leaning against the gates with a gaggle of girls that all look like pop stars or big sisters and I just look small and flea-like. They all laugh when I walk towards them, and I'm sure it isn't about me and walk past but when I look back they are looking at me and giggling even more and Clementine is whispering and her eyes are on me. I start running through my brain all the things that could be funny about me today . . . my hair – maybe the plait looks stupid and try-hard, maybe I have toothpaste on my chin? It's probably these stupid Dompy shoes, to be honest. I feel clown-like and sore-thumb-ish. How has Clementine made friends *already*? I know that American accent does all the hard work for her, that and the fact her mum buys her designer handbags. What's she got to keep inside them bags, anyway . . . felt tips? It's annoying she doesn't have to *try* like me. I might move to America for the opposite effect, even if it does mean eating plastic cheese.

I've also noticed that boys and girls don't really *hang* out with each other so much in this school either; it's not like small school where everybody blends in like kittens and it doesn't matter who you are, you all just snuggle in. I bet Will has noticed this too. I wonder if he will want to spend lunch time with me even though I forgot to ask Mum for burger money and have to eat Dad's packed sandwich?

I hurry to the meeting which is in the library – I can't wait to escape there, as books *never* judge you. The library is not how I thought it would be at all. In my head I pictured the local library near my house which is sticky and plain and the books all have tacky tape around the spine and the floor is all squeaky and the blinds have tea stains on them (and I even once saw a deaded mouse behind the A–D section in the fiction bookcase but I just mumbled 'oh dear' to myself and went to look in the religious section to perhaps find a prayer and read it to the mouse, but then I decided not to because all the words were way too hard in all the books).

But this isn't that at all. The staircase is huge and wooden and bold like a princess staircase, with a big sweeping balcony fenced the whole way around the top. The windows are stained glass in thousands of mighty glorious colours and shadows, and paint magical scenes onto the carpet below when the sun shines through. The books are well looked after and sleep in their own little shelves: it feels warm in here, safe and cosy and as quiet as actual silence. I finally feel like I can breathe. The idea of the meeting cheers me up a bit.

Mrs Ixy isn't there because students run the magazine, so instead there is a massive giant girl with a big chunky fringe and pink braces on who I think is in charge.

'Hi,' she beams and I curl up a bit from the sudden sound of her voice. 'It's OK, we can talk in here today. I know you're not *meant* to talk in libraries but they know we're having a meeting.' She introduces herself as 'Nicola, but everybody calls me Koala because I am sleepy and cuddly'. *I won't be doing any of that Koala-calling business*, I think to myself, but obviously I do because I don't want to upset this leader, who calls herself The Editor.

Koala (Nicola) sits at the head of the table – her legs are so long they are running underneath the table like sewage pipes. She introduces the rest of the team.

There is Gus, he is the Assistant Editor. He is OK but his nails are really very dirty like he is always digging up plants. His teeth are too sharp for a human; I am wondering why he wasn't given the chance of being a dinosaur instead of a boy.

Maggie, who is in charge of crosswords, puzzles and quizzes, is really cute and her nose in upturned like an imp. She has curly hair in bunches and lots of pen drawn all over her hands in designs and words.

Arti is in charge of artwork. Arti is very quiet but I can see her pad of paper and it is full of drawings of quite stunning things like stars and eyes. Wish I could draw like that, although if I was an amazing drawer I'd be drawing things like moose wearing bikinis rather than stars, I suspect.

And then Oliver (Olly) Supperidge. Even after just one meeting

I can officially announce that he is my new best person to not like and here's why. EVERYTHING that anybody says during the whole meeting he has to argue with or challenge or disagree with for no other reason than he enjoys watching others squirm their way out of his nasty traps, like bugs under a glass.

So Koala suggests that I talk to the group about who I am and what I've written in the past and my favourite book. The whole time Olly is rolling his eyes and tutting and deep sighing and he keeps looking behind my head to see if anybody more cooler or interesting is walking into the library.

Koala can see that Olly's behaviour is very rude and says, 'Erm, Olly, if you haven't noticed, Darcy's talking.'

And then Olly goes, 'Agh, soz' (as if that's a real way to apologize) and then he stretches back into his chair and overdramatically yawns, and during this stinky yawn says, 'Darcy, you don't even have a portfolio. I mean, you're still basically a kid, what have you actually *done*?' He is being really nasty and trying to expose me but before I can answer he talks about the *feel* of the magazine and starts using all these posh expensive words like 'contempt' and I think that alienates (which means to make people feel like the odd one out like an alien) our readers. If I ever got a chance to meet an alien I would never leave them out, I would *properly* hang out with them, not even forced.

Koala frowns at Olly and smiles her braces at me – they sparkle. 'Why don't we all ask Darcy a question about what we can look forward to with her being involved in the school mag?' Koala really enjoys speaking like a teacher. She asks, hoping to break the ice, 'Olly, why don't you kick us off?'

Olly finds it hard not to be rude. He laughs and then chews the end of his pen. Leaning on the back legs of his chair he sniffs and says, 'Personally I find this question near impossible to frame because I would much rather we were welcoming a male writer to the magazine.'

'A boy?' Maggie squeals.

I snarl. *What's the difference?* I can't believe my ears.

Maggie glares at Olly. 'What do you mean? A boy writer, why?'

'Well, I think my articles have completely smashed

it, I mean, I've set the bar pretty high, I know I'm writing stuff that people want to read and I'm worried that a female writer might . . . you know . . . lower the standard of the magazine, like I don't think they will want to read a *beauty* column or to hear about stupid ponies and baking and the colour pink.'

'I'm sure some people would like to hear about that sort of stuff, but luckily for you, Olly, I don't think that's exactly what Darcy had in mind, was it, Darcy?' Koala asks me. Her eyes are so wide right now it's like they might drop out of their sockets, rolling onto the carpet, collecting up dirt and hairs.

The room feels numb and almost a bit hysterical but I am not confident or comfortable enough to start giggling. I feel sorry for Olly that he thinks girls aren't as good as boys, he will certainly be growing up to be one of those idiot men that says 'women can't drive' or 'a woman's place is in the kitchen'. My dad would NEVER EVER think like that or else he would get his head chopped off with Mum's toenail clippers. I say loud and proud, 'I write about stuff that inspires me . . . you never know, Olly, you might make it into a story yourself one of these days.'

Koala (Nicola) is explaining that our next big magazine is the autumn issue. It will be celebrating the new school year, welcoming the newcomers and catching up with what happened over summer. She also lets me know that they've been working on the magazine through the summer holiday (as they are all year above) and this is the first time a Year Seven has participated, the deadline is short and so she 'completely understands' if I haven't got the time to contribute this issue and could write something for the next one.

It's too late for me; I'm so inspired by the idea of autumn that my head is already cooking something up . . . what better than a dark story for autumn? I am imagining a reader curled up in front of a fire preparing for the winter, the leaves dancing outside, a mug of hot chocolate (but you say cocoa instead because that makes you want it more) and a blanket, maybe a Lamb-Beth there to sit and stroke. Yes, a nice dark story.

'I want to do it!' I blurt out.

'You sure?' Maggie says. 'I know you guys get loads of homework in the first year.'

'Hmm . . . if you can call writing your name on exercise books "homework"!' Olly sniggers, and does those stupid bunny ear speech marks with his fingertips when he says the word 'homework'.

'I want to. I write lots at home so it won't make a difference. I am going to write a story,' I say, thinking aloud.

'Great, Darcy! Welcome to the team!'

'What's this story about?' Olly grunts. Jealous.

'Some sisters!' I improvise.

Olly and his humungous ego can't let this one go. 'Family stories are kind of . . . well . . . old-fashioned – people like to read about football, celebrities and politics.' He leans back into his chair, stretching his arms over his head, thinking that's what people do in meetings. The whole table looks to me.

'I think that is not true, Olly. People have got imaginations too and the only thing I find truly old-fashioned is to believe that girls can't do stuff that boys can actually.' I blush.

'This is just frustrating,' he scoffs. 'I don't have the time for this garbage. You are writing a story about *girly sisters* – unbelievable. Stick with that attitude and your story will be . . . pretty . . . dumb.'

PRETTY DUMB? PRETTY DUMB? I am scowling.

'We will see about that, Olly.' I lift my head and raise my brows. I feel like an actor.

'We will,' he grunts, all cocky like he believes himself to be James Bond.

The pressure is on.

The bell rings for first lesson and the meeting dissolves to an end, Koala pats me on the shoulder, grinning, and lisps, 'Great start, Darcy,' showering me in little flicks of spit that I don't wipe off obviously, as Mum brought me up properly. I smile back and try to ignore Olly packing his bag furiously and dramatically before grunting as he bowls out of the library. I hope I haven't just taken on too much.

The rest of the morning I live in my own head flicking through scenes of my new story like a comic book, zoning in and out of real life and interrupting my own ideas. Inspiration works best like this.

I am on smiling and hello terms with nearly everybody in my class and finally manage to grab a seat next to Will in French.

'Where were you this morning?' he whispers.

'I had a meeting.' I bite my lip, all excited.

'A *meeting*? What about? Were you in trouble with Mrs Ixy?'

'I thought I was, but no! Phew, it's good news, they want me to write for the school magazine!'

Will's quiet for a moment and doesn't say anything, but it's almost as though I can hear his insides churning. He carries on scribbling away in his book, pretending to look busy.

'That's really good,' he whispers back. 'Well done.' He finishes and then weirdly shifts his body away from me with his head in his hand and starts paying attention to the French class. I peep over his shoulder to see what he's written and it just says *NO. NO. NO. NO. NO. NO. NO,* over and over again, and a heap of scribbles. I don't know why.

I try not to worry about Will's odd behaviour and let myself drift off to the writing book in my head, allowing myself to drift in and out of real land and daydream land at the drop of a hat; allow myself to pass time by whirling away in my head and scribbling and scrawling and imagining and creating and writing as much as I can. Building together my story.

The first half of the day flutters by so fast that I can't believe it's lunch time when the bell rings. Will waits around in the classroom for me to go to the canteen with him but I've got so much work to do.

'You ready?' He grins. 'I've got money, look, let's hope they've got burgers again!'

'Aargh, Will, I've got a sandwich today, I forgot to get money off Mum, and then Dad had already made it and . . . but I think I might actually eat it in the library and get this story for the magazine done. If that's OK?'

Will stutters, looks like his face has melted off.

'Sure, I'll just . . . I'll just see what some of the boys are doing.'

'Is that cool?' I say, knowing it isn't and it is a bit selfish of me; it is only day two and I am already abandoning Will to that cafeteria.

'Course. See you later, hope you get lots done.'

'You too!' I say back, pleased that I am clearly not completely wrapped up in myself.

Maggie is in the library too. We write stupid notes to each other and draw pictures of the annoying

librarian and before we know it lunch has ended and I didn't do any writing whatsoever, just hung out with Maggie when I could have hung with Will.

After a day of me avoiding all lesson-learning by writing, Will and I are walking out of that very schoolish building and he is being a very thoughtful person and asking me lots about my new job as a journalist and what I am writing about, which is pretty pleasant. I explain that even though it's for the magazine I am getting to write my own short story and it gets to be fictional which means made up in my own brain. I would find facts too hard and strict, and obviously I pretend I had done lots of writing in the library, not messing around with Maggie.

It's nice catching up with Will, and then out of nowhere dreaded toxic Clementine struts over with her stupid long tussled but not knotty hair and long legs.

'Will!' she smiles, all American and fake. Will repels and coils a little, curls up like a little prawn trapped inside a folding deckchair. I put my hands on my hips, ready to blaze her if necessary – but she seems to ignore me completely as though I'm a ghost that only Will can see. 'It's my birthday next week and I'm taking ten LUCKY friends to a really posh restaurant in central London and then for ice cream after. The restaurant is so nice, they serve everything

on big white plates, would you like to come?'

DO I NOT EXIST? Not that I would have wanted to celebrate idiot annoying Clementine's birthday, but *really* . . . I mean, talk about ill timing. Will won't say yes anyway, I'm thinking, he knows better than to say yes to that slug.

Will rolls his sleeves up, giving himself something to do before he whacks her with the big 'NO'. But instead he smiles and says, 'Yeah, sure, when is it?'

My jaw drops. WHAT? Have I been in a coma for the last year? I try to hide the shock from my face but I just can't.

Clementine screeches and grabs his hand. I think my nostrils flare. 'Next Saturday, I'll bring in details tomorrow, great, catch ya later.'

NO, not 'CATCH YA LATER!' Not 'CATCH YA LATER' *AT ALL*! Clementine strolls off, flicking her hair, her (far too short) skirt flapping in the wind and her BEAUTIFUL school shoes making her look like a model and not like a me and my Dompy terrible feet.

Will looks a bit happy with himself. *How did they become friends then? What have I missed?* Then I see the big graze on Will's elbow.

'What's that from?' I point to the new bloody scab.

'Football. I played at lunch time.'

Oh, you did, did ya? Hmmm. The plot thickens.

I bet Will scored a goal and Clementine ran over and smooched him in front of everybody and now they are in love and getting married and I'll have to cope my whole life with being friends with Will but also having to put up with that beast brute Clementine every minute. I'll have to go and visit their house in the country and bring them lemon drizzle cake to celebrate their new life when secretly I hate them. OR, what if she forces him to go and live in the UNITED STATES OF AMERICA with her? She might kidnap him and he won't ever want to see me and Lamb-Beth ever again? Then I realize I'm getting carried away and feel guilty. There was me going on and on about myself and I hadn't asked him ANYTHING about himself.

'Did you score a goal?' I ask, a bit wanting him to be rubbish at football so he doesn't feel tempted to do something without me again.

'Yeah, three! A hat trick – they put me on their shoulders!'

'They didn't?' I gasp. I feel sick. I can't believe I

missed this. I can just imagine how happy that would have made him and I wasn't there to see it.

I know Will too well, but just to try and wake up his delusional brain I say, 'So when are you going to tell Clementine that you're obviously NOT going to her birthday party at the *posh blah blah restaurant with the big white plates*?' I imitate her stupid American accent.

'What? I *am* going. I want to.'

'Yeah, right.'

'No, really, I want to.'

'OK, but only to eat the snobby food then?'

'No, I like her. She came to watch me play today, she cheered me on, we spoke, she's cool, she's not like *that* any more. People change, Darcy.'

Stupid mature gross forgiving but also naïve Will liking horrid poo-face Clementine. I feel guilty and lefted out and upset and regretful for going to the library when really I should have been with Will and then he never would have gone and played any stupid football and would not have changed his mind about Clementine.

I think I should say something funny from our past to remind Will that I am his all-time best friend, but then I hear, 'Darcy!' from behind me. It's Maggie, with her big curly bunches and happy face.

'Who's that?' Will whispers under his breath, but I don't have time to answer because Maggie has

launched in on the magazine and saying a squillion things and won't stop being excited. I think Will might be looking a bit at Maggie like, *Who is this out-of-control girl that Darcy has latched onto?* But I can't help but want to be excited back by Maggie.

Before I even know it, Will runs over to Annie's car and gets inside and we didn't even get a chance to catch up properly. He waves me off. *Why do I feel guilty about that?* He's the annoying one for being new best friends forever with Clementine; it should be HIM feeling guilty – not me . . . then again I guess I'm the one that left him to fend for himself at lunch time, turning down his burger money.

Mum pulls up next to me, Poppy and Hector already in the car looking all like 'our school is so easy for babies and yours is tough and tricky and hard and scary'. *Shut up, you idiots, anyway.*

Mum pulls into the electrical shop to do I don't know what. This is maybe our most favourite place on the planet. It is a big shop full of televisions all on the same channel which makes your mind go upside-down into mad chaos and then all these stereos plugged in singing the same song. But the truly best bit about the electrical shop is the kitchen section. I mean, it is out of control with brilliance.

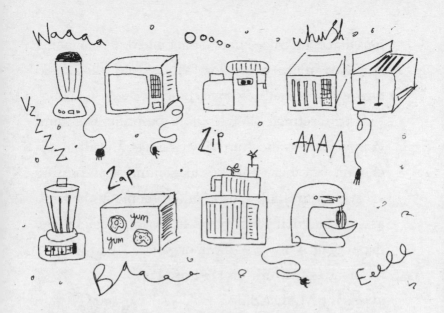

Thousands of different designed fridges that you can open and close, blenders, microwaves, cookers, freezers, toasters, mixers, ice-cube makers, waffle machines, doughnut machines . . . even a candyfloss maker. Back in the day, when we were younger, our natural instinct was to *play house*. Poppy always got to play Mum and I had to be the dad but to be honest I was sick of that boring game: there are only so many times I could be bothered to pretend to forget to put the toilet seat down or '*make a cup of coffee*'

plus that deep voice I had to put on to be a convincing dad gave me a really sore sandy itchy throat. So now we do something *much* cooler.

The electrical shop is now basically *space* and Poppy, Hector and I are space cadets. Usually I am captain, but that's only because I am best at bossing everybody around. All the other people in the shop are either enemy aliens or fellow crew members, depending if we like the look of them or not. Mum or Dad are *always* the Mother Ship.

Lots can happen up in *space*. Whether or not that's killing a forceful wall of a bazillion green four-eyed monster aliens or simply cruising in the cockpit, there is always work to be done. My most favourite thing to do, however, when in space, is to run around panicking, pressing every single button and gadget I can find in the electrical shop and quickly saying every single slightly technical or complicated sounding word I can imagine.

'Vortex, download a rechargeable disk, countdown vortex zero, hard-drive expandable data chips, field and Internet connection, I can't get a signal. Collect your bearings, send down the printout, steer the body of the ship over to the homeland. Connect, troops over the system, we've got to go now!! Officer Poppy, second in command, press the red button over there on the squasher, you know what the squasher is' (the blender). 'There must be a life force out there, Officer Hector, third in command. You're the only one I trust on this ship if Poppy and I don't make it back in time, you've always been brave and hard-working. If the ship doesn't make it back or the gravity is rooting back to the electronic chamber of death, you *know* what to do. For now, watch the DVD doesn't rotate into the iPad and destroy all previous account numbers and sim cards. For now, know that I honour you. Vortex, all systems on lockdown, punishing the universe with this microwave on voltage wave in five . . . four . . . three . . . two . . . one. Release,' I say as I cling onto the hand-held electric whisk, close my eyes and hold my breath. I think *Vortex* is my favourite word in this game.

Chapter Nine

It's been a whole week now, and the school magazine job is getting busier and busier, and like Dad's job it sometimes has to come home with me. I haven't been free to have fun and see Will, even though I'm worrying that Clementine may be his new best friend it's just a risk I'm having to take to make sure I get everything done. He seems fine, he plays football and stuff, plus he's clever so I'm sure his brain is getting fed. I am working like a dog (heard Dad say this), even though I don't why people say they are *working like a dog* as all I ever see dogs doing is sleeping, eating and sniffing each other's bums. Especially Kevin, Henrietta-from-next-door's dog.

 I have visited Kevin a few times – he's a bulldog with bright red eyes and a jaw like the tray you put the paper into in the school printer when it's jammed. He walks like a gorilla and he slobbers all over everything. He came from a rescue centre so I think he's got issues so I often steer out of his way in case one day he decides to take those *issues* out on my leg. For now he just, as I said, sleeps, eats and sniffs bums.

Cyril pops over, which is annoying as I just want to write, and he wants a cup of coffee and to keep telling my mum that 'there are no hard feelings' about his arm being broked. A hard feeling is whcn somebody is giving you the brushoff because you've been horrid. First I'm mad, but then I think it's generous of Cyril not to give us any of his hard feelings. I really don't want them and besides I have nowhere to store them, my room is a tip. Cyril also has a sling. It looks like a nappy, with a big pin. I keep staring at it. We say 'thanks and everything for the seeds'. Even though we can't even plant them as the weather is still not good. He should have just got us Maltesers. We say goodbye and I settle down to write with a cup of hot chocolate.

The door goes again. 'I'll get it!' I roar up the stairs. In my head I'm hoping it is Cyril to say, 'Sorry, I lost my mind and almost forgot to give you these, what was I thinking?' and hand me a sack of Maltesers, but it's not, it's Will. His bike is on the pavement next to him, the wheels still spinning from how fast he must have rode here. Will is really good at changing into his own clothes after the school day is done whereas I can never be bothered. He looks as though he has even *washed* too and put fresh gel in his hair.

'Oh.' My face falls; he will be wanting to spend time with me now but I've got writing to do.

'Gosh, don't seem *too* happy to see me,' he laughs with sarcasm, and before I can defend myself he pulls out a DVD from his jacket. 'I stole this horror film from Annie's room. I've heard there's zombies in it.'

He grins and goes to walk inside. Lamb-Beth tilts her head at him.

'Sorry, Will, not tonight, I've got lots of stuff to—'

'I get it,' he says. 'Don't worry, you have been really busy these days.' He looks upsetted.

'OK, I'm sure we—'

'Don't worry about it, honestly.' He turns away, leaps on his BMX and rides away faster that I can shout 'STOP' – maybe that's because I didn't want him to stop, I'm not even sure. As I shut the door, I manage to capture Mum's curious face in the reflection of the glass.

That was silly of me. I think about how much I regretted not spending time with him before, and how I didn't even see him over the weekend, and now I've just ruined my chance to see him now. I go back to the kitchen where my hot chocolate has already gone cold. I look depressed. I can tell.

'How's Will finding new school, monkey? Hope he's getting on all right,' Mum says, as she defaces the picture of an actress in one of her magazines, giving her a unibrow, blacked-out teeth and glasses. This has annoyed me because I know she is trying to dissect my brain and work out why Will and I aren't being as close as normally.

'He's fine,' I say and then carry on writing.

'Do you spend much time with him at school?' she asks me. 'Or just mostly with this Maggie girl from the magazine?'

'What's Maggie got to do with anything?' I snap. I am just stressed from starting big school and joining the magazine, and maybe also it's because she's right and Will and I have a little rip in our friendship. ONLY a little one.

'All right, sorry, I didn't mean to ruffle your feathers.' I imagine myself as a giant exotic bird with an angry face and multi-coloured feathers being blown about in the wind.

I feel like I have to defend my actions to myself.

Maggie is the year above me and her days are different to mine, so sometimes she even calls me on the house phone after school, which is very strange for me and makes Poppy look at me like 'WHO DO YOU THINK YOU ARE?' but really I know she's just jealous. Mum and Dad are proud of me, I think, and I've seen Dad smile when the phone rings and Mum shouts, 'Darcy, it's for you!' They keep telling me to invite Maggie over for Chinese takeaway or Mum's wretched fish pie, but I feel weird to ask because she's in the year above me and anyway she's not my BEST friend, Will is. Everybody knows you're not meant to be BEST friends with people in the year below or above. Then again, everybody seems to be thinking it's pretty weird that I'm best friends with a boy.

I shake my head and start writing again but I can't do it. If I'm going to get this story finished I need to push all my real-life worries to the back of my head or deal with them. I'm not that good at pushing things to the back of my head. Mum's right. Will hasn't been over for takeaway or wretched fish pie for the longest time in the history of us being mates. I think probably I should work on making Will more importanter in my life once again, and so for the first time in all our lives I am going to pick up the phone and call *him*. I punch in the numbers and wait on the line.

Annie picks up.

'Hiya, Annie, it's Darcy, is Will please in?' I tumble the words out so quick like I am a rattlesnake.

' 'Allo, Darcy, yeah, I think so. Hold on . . . *Ginger Nut*!' she calls up the stairs. Annie is the only person in the world who Will lets call him Ginger Nut. It's funny, it's a bit like how you can call your sister a bajillion words under the sun but the moment somebody else is mean about her, then you want to plunge a sword through their belly.

'Hello?' His voice is all low like he has turned into a shy person.

'Hi, Will. It's me, Darcy.'

'Yeah, I know.'

What on earth do people say when they are on the phone? 'So, erm, how are you?'

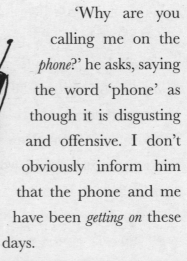

'Why are you calling me on the *phone*?' he asks, saying the word 'phone' as though it is disgusting and offensive. I don't obviously inform him that the phone and me have been *getting on* these days.

'Well, why not?' I ask, taken aback. I wasn't expecting that.

'It's weird. Why can't we just speak at school? I thought you were busy anyway.'

'That's why I was calling actually – we haven't

really seen each other much . . .'

'That's why I came over, you doughnut. To hang out. Look, it's not a big deal. I know you are busy, you being a writer, and that's what you want, isn't it?'

'Yes . . . but . . .'

'So what's the problem?'

'There's no problem.'

'Fine.'

'Fine.' I swallow to the back of my throat and it tastes like *horrible*. My tongue is like a giant cream cracker, dry and plain. It feels so awkward. Why does 'no problem' scream 'BIG PROBLEM'. I knewed we weren't speaking to each other but I didn't realize that there was an actual real-life problem bubbling between us. I panic.

'What are you having for dinner?' I ask. In moments of terror always resort to food, unless there is none about and then chew your hair.

'Takeaway pizza.'

'Oh, lucky.'

There is a frosty pause.

'I'll bring you in a slice tomorrow if you want.'
Phew.

'That would be really good.' I smile to myself.

'I've got a football match at lunch time. It's a big one, against the older boys, if you want to watch.'

'Yes, yes, I would love to. I'll be there.'

'OK, bye. Don't ring again, it's weird, I don't like it.'

'Sorry, I won't. I don't like it either.' Which isn't true. I love the phone.

'Fine.'

'Fine.'

'Bye then.'

'Bye.'

Then we hang up the phone. Well, that went well. At least I can be sure that we are still mates. He is bringing me pizza and I am going to watch him play football at lunch, and even if that rogue Clementine is there I will simply have to just be mature about it like a stinky old lump of cheese. I am a really good friend. I am a REALLY good friend. I AM REALLY good at being a REALLY GOOD friend. I brush my hair, which I have been doing a bit since I am a journalist, and get Mum to re-plait it all nice and neat for me. I work on my story really hard and think it's finished and I feel happy with it and Dad helps me put the story on a posh little keyring thing that means I can take the story to school and work on the same document tomorrow. Sadly I can't write everything in my own writing book. I watch a bit of *The Simpsons* with Poppy and Hector, burping up my dinner as loud as I can to nearly the whole theme tune, which is making them laugh, and then I'm nearly a bit sick so I stop.

I lie in bed with my hand around Lamb-Beth's ear. I am humming. I think about picking my nose but that's gross and I figure if I don't pick my nose by this age it's probably not a good time to start a disgusting new habit. I dream . . .

Through the twinkly sky the light shades fades every colour and a gentle humming noise finds Will, in the centre of the ocean, on a boat rocking. It is

calm and peaceful. I am a mermalade (magical like a mermaid and normal like marmalade = mermalade – obviously) and I am flapping about beside the boat but still in the water and sharing some tacos and pizza with Will, and because we are expert at this none of the tacos or pizza get wet. We then play some table tennis and it's going well because we are pretty much the same level of good at table tennis. Then suddenly, out of nowhere, a terribly scary and awful storm brews. A storm that thunders and lightning and the sky gets all dark and stormy and the birds are swooping and the trees surrounding are blowing and rattling and a white brilliant light is flashing over up and crackling and cackling and the sea gets more choppy and starts sucking me under, and even though I'm a mermalade my normal abilities seem to be dominating my magical mythical ones and I begin to drown.

I panic and my hair is so swampy and heavy I can barely lift my head. I can't breathe and then the sea trembles and monsters come, huge big oily ones with ginormous big tails and talons, and whipping lashing furious sounds are groaning out of them and I am screaming and Will keeps trying to tip me up into his boat and scoop me in, but I keep slipping – it's as though my skin is covered in butter and I keep dipping back into the water. Instead of helping me stay afloat my tail is like a dead weight now, dragging me down, and the more I try to swim the more the water becomes thick and stiffens like custard. Will can't grip me!

The monster is snaking closer and the sky is thick and heavy like a stew pot of smoke tipping on our heads and the water begins to swirl, and at the last moment Will finally manages to pull me up and into the boat and we are yelling and out of breath and soaking wet and crying, and just when we think we are safe, suddenly the boat tips, capsizes us . . . and I wake up, panting, with hot tears streaming down my face.

Chapter Ten

The next morning Will is doing his *looking like I'm not but I am waiting for you look* at the gates with a bunch of tinfoil in his hands. This will be my delicious pizza, I think. He hands it to me.

'Pepperoni.' He smiles. He has orange-juice breath. I wonder if he brushed his teeth because everybody knows that toothpaste mixed with orange juice makes revolting acid.

'Yummy. Thanks, Will.'

'You still coming to watch me play football today?'

'Of course. I can't wait.'

'Cool, you don't have to, you know, if you're busy or whatever.'

'No, I want to.' AS IF I'm going to let Clementine have that smug grin all over her face AGAIN – I don't think so!

'Cool.' He looks pleased and then walks away.

'Good luck!' I call after him. *We are friends again.*

The day goes so fast, and even though I am in lessons I keep thinking about how the magazine deadline is tomorrow ALREADY, and if I'm going to get my story in this first edition I have to hurry up and edit this stupid thing. This is much more stressful than writing my own little stories in my writing book. There is so much to do, every spare second I have I spend in the computer room with Maggie, Gus, Arti and Koala typing away like mad. I also know my spelling and grammar is bad ugly and have to try really hard at making sure it is a good piece of work, and all that tidying up is NOT my strong point. Olly has handed in all his written work so I haven't seen him much, but this doesn't stop him leering over my computer screen at break time for a good five minutes.

'Erm, Darcy, an apostrophe goes before the "s" when it *belongs* to somebody,' he snoots, rubbing his greasy hands on my screen.

I smile and say, 'Thanks.'

'You're welcome,' he chimes. 'We can't *all* be fortunate enough to be as clever as I am.' I roll my eyes, watching him do some stretches and rubbing his chin. He is playing in the football match at lunch time – apparently he is a 'big deal' – and I wish he would hurry up and leave.

'I should be the punctuation police, cracking down on all those slippery apostrophes. It's not really your fault, Darcy,' he snipes, glaring at his reflection in the window. He licks his fingers and spreads the spit over his eyebrows, shaping them

134

into horrible mountain points. 'You have to have the *knack* for it, I simply can't imagine what the ratio is of people that ARE writers in comparison to people who WANT to be writers but will never get the chance, purely because simple things like bad grammar or laziness lets them down.' He shrugs. 'Ah, *c'est la vie.*' IS HE SPEAKING FRENCH NOW? *Really?*

Maggie whispers in my ear, 'Pretentious.' I don't know what that means either but I giggle anyway because her tone lets me know she thinks he's a twit.

Luckily for me, Olly air-punches the ceiling a few times, mooches around and then slumps out of the computer room to play football. I can't be bothered to row with him. I didn't even agree with a single word he just said but sneakily Google *c'est la vie* just to see. It means 'such is life'. I speak English and *still* have NO idea what that means either. Oh, great.

I have a brisk ten minutes before Will's football

match where I can get up to the computer room and have one final read of my story before deadline. Then I can eat the pizza Will gave me and cheer him on during his game. Maggie is sitting there when I arrive.

'Hi,' I pant when I plonk myself down next to her.

'Your story looks great – want one final read and make any changes?' she squeals.

'That's why I'm here, yes please.'

The Craggle Twins

They lived five doors apart at the top of a steep stalk of a hill: the Craggle Twins. Their relationship was one of the most fussy and complicated relationships ever known in the dizzy tapestry of relationships because they loved and hated each other exactly to the same degree. They couldn't live together but they couldn't

live apart. Their names were Cora and Dora and they were both middle-aged. They had long-to-the-ground knotty scraggly hair, really skinny bony arms and legs, with big fat round bodies. They looked like boiled eggs with four toothpicks stuck into them as limbs. They had the same interests, hobbies and tastes.

Their interest was gerbils, their hobby was stuffing the gerbils once they had died, and their taste was eating tinned fish. They had never had a boyfriend because whenever one met a man she liked, the other would find a way to destruct and destroy the other's bliss. They were quite happy in their loneliness, well, they had to be, they wouldn't let each other have any happiness so they had to have each other. That was until the new postman came. Dave. Simple, unibrowed, toothless Dave.

Cora's house was first on the route, number 19. He had a parcel of stuffing for Cora to continue her hobby with those poor gerbils, and took quite a fancy to this miserable-looking dollop of a woman, in her lilac nightie and her hair rolled into little mini pigs in blankets. She liked the idea of a handsome postman called Dave being her boyfriend, and couldn't help but scrape her needle fingers over his soft hands as they exchanged the parcel for a signature before saying, 'Cheerio.' The smell of dead gerbil and sardines followed him down the road. 'I fancy that Dave,' she said to herself as she closed her net curtains. 'And I think he fancies me too!' But there was one problem: Dora.

Cora was near certain her twin sister would have the hots for Postman Dave just as she did and dreaded what would happen when he paid Dora a call . . .

Knock, knock, knock. It was the new postman, Dave, with the package of stuffing that Dora too had ordered. When she opened the door of number 24, it was love at first

sight for Dora, but *déjà vu* for Dave. He was
shocked and he shook his head. *Hadn't he seen*
all this before? The attractive woman, the smell
of dead gerbil and sardine all on the same road
no more than two minutes ago? Still, it was
nice to see her again and he was so simple he
soon got over it. Dora couldn't help but flick her
knotty hair over her shoulder and breathe her
fishy breath over Dave with a lovestruck smile.

Cora peered out of her window and saw

Postman Dave leaving Dora's house. She had to put a stop to this and quick. Meanwhile Dora knew that Cora lived at number 19, so she must have been visited by hunky Dave before her. That meant that she technically found him before her. *Finders keepers*. She had to do something.

Both Craggle twins wrapped themselves up in their mustard corduroy coats and headed to the other's house 'for tea and a bun'. But they ended up meeting in the middle of the street, at number 22.

'What do you want?' Dora grunted.

'Same as you,' Cora sneered.

'What's that then?' Dora frowned.

'You tell me,' Cora smirked.

'I was coming to see you.' Dora lifted her voice in high fakery.

'Me too,' Cora chimed.

'What for?' Dora sniffed.

'Bun and tea,' Cora curled.

'How delightful,' Dora spat.

'And you?' Cora gritted her teeth.

'The same . . .' Dora held her tongue.

'Well . . .' they said together, 'aren't you going to invite me in?'

They stood hawking over each other before they both said, again, at the same time, 'Hands off, he's mine!' and then they gasped and screwed their faces up.

'I saw him first!' Cora cried. 'Finders keepers.'

Dora snickered. 'I'm inviting him over,' she barked.

'Me too!' snaked Cora.

'Then we'll see who he likes best!' announced Dora.

'Yes we will, you pesky hag!' pronounced Cora.

'You wretched worm!'

'You cabbaged caked cod!'

'You man-nicking knicker head!'

'You boyfriend-boasting beastly bum bum beef burger!'

'You horrible handsome-husband hovering hacking hole in my head!'

'I WISH YOU WERE DEAD!' they roared in unison, huffed and stropped back to their own houses. This meant war.

They both had the same tactic: if they were going to invite Postman Dave inside for a date the first thing they had to do was get him to deliver them a package. It couldn't be a letter because a postman doesn't knock for a letter so they both ordered a big box of

143

stuffing to be delivered the next day.

However, Dora knew that Cora would be ordering something for Postman Dave to deliver, same as her, so she needed to do a little something else, just to make sure her sister's date didn't go quite as smoothly. Dora ordered 500 tablets of a special medicine that makes someone stop farting so much. She ordered them to be delivered to her twin sister's house the very next morning, knowing full well that Postman Dave would see the box and think Dora was a Problem Farter. 'Hee. Hee. Hee,' she cackled to herself and said 'Stupid Cora' to her stuffed gerbils, to which the stuffed gerbils said nothing.

Knock, knock, knock, at number 19. *Was it that time already?* Cora sprang up from the couch and dusted herself down. It was Postman Dave. He was happy to see her and wriggled his unibrow and gaped at her with his toothless grin.

'Delivery for Miss C. Craggle: one box of

stuffing.' He handed her the box and she did the hand touchy thing again, thanked him and smiled, thinking that this would be the right moment to invite him in. But Dave picked up another box, 'Ooh, busy day for you, Miss Craggle, you have another box here . . . five hundred tablets of Fart Killer?' Dave tried to keep a straight face but he wanted to laugh.

'That's not mine!' Cora hissed.

'Well, it's got your name on it,' Dave replied.

'WHO ORDERED THESE?'

'Not sure, I'm just doing my job, Miss Craggle.'

And suddenly she knew *exactly* who had ordered them. Her sister, Dora. This was *serious*. Cora said goodbye to Dave: the moment was gone, the date was now ruined. Now she had to ruin her sister's chances too.

Meanwhile, five doors down, Dora was wearing a very-too-small-for-herself dress, her pale skin pouring out in big fat fleshy folds. She thought she looked great and couldn't wait to answer the door to Postman Dave, especially now her sister would be out of the picture thanks to the fart tablets. He would be coming any minute, she thought as she drank the last of the tuna oil at the bottom of the can, waiting for the knock at the door.

But it didn't come.

Eventually she opened the front door, and saw Dave's postman van speeding away. She was furious and completely confused, but then she noticed her door numbers had been swapped around to read '42' rather than the correct '24' and Postman Dave (being not the smartest cookie in the cookie jar) had simply driven right past her house. Only someone with a brain as deadly as her own could achieve such a trick: Cora.

She picked up the phone and telephoned her sister.

'Cora speaking,' Cora cooed before she knew it was her sister.

'It's me,' Dora grunted. 'We have to invite Postman Dave over, together, at the same time, so there's no funny business and we can't ruin it for each other with nasty tricks. It's the only way we can be sure which one he likes the best.'

'Fine.'

'Great.'

'Perfect.'

'Wonderful.'

And they both hung up the phone.

As Cora's house was first on Postman Dave's route they decided to hold the date there, at number 19. Both sisters would have a job to do. Cora was to prepare the sandwiches and Dora was to prepare the entertainment. They had ordered more stuffing to arrive sharp the next morning.

Here they were, in Cora's living room, full of stuffed gerbils, pigs and weird ornaments. They sat drinking tea, not speaking, just communicating

by the occasional arched eyebrow or body
twitch, their knobbly knees rattling, their round
bellies quivering with anticipation, until the door
knocked.

'I'll get it!' they sang together, but began
elbowing each other out of the way, stepping on
each other's faces, forcing and squeezing their
way to the front door — a ridiculous scramble
of grey clothes and fish breath.

'Coming!' Cora chirped, trying to sound breezy
before kicking her sister in the shin.

Dora winced and then gritted her teeth. 'Just
a moment!' she tinkled and clawed Cora's face,
causing her to silently
scream.

Until they opened
the door, together,
and met the
blank gaze
of Postman
Dave.

'I have a delivery here for . . .' And then he looked up, stunned. How could so much beauty be in one house at one time? They were either twin sisters or this was a dream that he never wanted to end. They invited him in for tea and he, of course, agreed and stepped inside. Work would have to wait.

'Tea, Mr Dave?' Cora asked, wiggling her bum and reaching for the teapot.

'Please,' Dave said. He was nervous and beads of sweat stood out on his forehead; he had never seen so many stuffed gerbils.

'I stuff them myself,' Cora said, smiling proudly.

'I do too,' Dora quickly added.

'Right . . .' Dave dropped a cube of sugar into his cup.

'Sandwich?' Cora passed Dave the plate of tinned fish sandwiches. 'There's tuna, salmon, sardine and anchovies. Help yourself, there's plenty more where that came from.' Cora smirked as Dave loaded his plate and then she gave the evil eye to her sister, carefully swinging the plate her way; Dora took a handful of sandwiches.

'Thank you.' Dave bit into his sandwich. 'Yum . . .' he forced out through a mouth of oil and bones. Cora began eating hers too and tried to eat all perfect but couldn't help it because she loved tinned fish sandwiches too much and rammed the whole thing down in one go like a sea serpent.

Dora lifted hers to her mouth, sniffing for poison (you never know) and began to eat hers too; the only noise was the chewing from the three of them. Once lunch was done the twins cleared the plates away in the kitchen whilst Dave sat, twiddling his thumbs in silence.

'How was lunch?' Cora asked her sister in a whisper, almost genuinely concerned to get things right.

'Fine.' Dora shrugged and then became a bit

softer. 'Good, it was nice, I enjoyed it,' she whispered back.

'That's good to know for your future budgeting: using cat food is much cheaper than tinned salmon. Your sarnies were all made from cat food, MEEEEEEOW!' Cora cackled before scuttling out to grab some alone time with Dave, leaving Dora rinsing her tongue out under the tap and retching; what a devil sister!

Dora had to get her own back. Entertainment was down to her and she had to seem as charming as she could, cat-food breath or not. They were going to watch a film. Perfect for some serious handholding!

'It's supposed to be hilarious!' Dora showed off.

'I love comedies,' said Postman Dave.

'Me too.' Cora wriggled up next to Dave on the couch.

'It says here you will go *blind with laughter*!' Dora was reading out the blurb on the back of the case. 'Let's hope not, eh?' she joked, and both her and Cora put their glasses on.

The film began and at every scene the sisters were laughing, close to hysterical; they had reached a new tier of over-excitement. Every time Dora laughed, Cora had to laugh harder, to show Dave she had a better sense of humour. Dave was sandwiched in the middle like a sausage inside their bums of white bread and was gently snorting.

'I'm just going to spend a penny,' Cora said as she nipped for a wee (because that's what older people say when they need to wee).

Whilst Cora was gone, Dora very sneakily and quietly took her glasses and, without Dave noticing, wiped them in the lip gloss she had been wearing, smearing the front of the lenses in thick gluey grime, making them near impossible to see through and everything a blur. She then placed the glasses back on the couch

and carried on finding everything side-splittingly
hilarious.

Cora waltzed back in. 'Miss me?' she pouted,
then put her glasses back on. She couldn't see a
thing. She tried to concentrate, wiggle her pupils;
did she have something inside her eye? Her
sister Dora was in hysterics even more now, but
not from the film.

'You OK, Cora?' Dora managed to ask.

'Yep,' Cora lied.

'Sure, Cora?' Dora probed.

'Well, there is something . . . I can't see . . .'
Cora freaked, 'anything, just swirling colour.'

'Oh dear!' Dora said, pretend-worriedly. 'It
does say the film is so funny you'll go *blind*
with laughter and you have been doing quite
a lot of laughing, haven't you? You should be
more careful next time!'

'Oh my goodness, you're right, I am blind,
I am as blind as a bat!' Cora started to
panic, she was screaming and yelling and

hyperventilating and her sister then panicked too — she hated Cora but she didn't want her to *die*. Dora reached over and grabbed the glasses off her sister's face. 'You're fine, see? It was just lip gloss!' she shouted.

'You let me think I was *blind*!' Cora wailed.

'You let me eat cat food!' Dora cried.

'You sent fart tablets to my house!' Cora bellowed.

'You swapped the numbers on my front door round!' Dora screamed and then REALLY screamed again, 'Oh no! Cora! Cora . . . we've killed Dave, we've squished him, look . . .'

And a flattened lilo of a man in a post office uniform slid down off the sofa, leaving the Craggle Twins staring at him through horrified tears.

I get to the last word and breathe a sigh of relief. It's done and I'm happy with it.

'Don't know what Olly was on about, your grammar is fine,' Maggie says, patting me on the back.

'Thanks,' I reply.

'Even if it isn't perfect, it doesn't matter: the story is what people will be interested in, not spelling mistakes.'

I go to press 'save' but suddenly the worserest thing in the whole of the universe happens. The lights go out in the computer room and then the darkness is followed by a slow grinding sound as all the computers flash off to dark screens.

'NO!'

'What's happened?' I shout, panic rising.

'Power cut, I think . . .'

'What does that mean?'

'It means our work could be lost.'

'No. It can't be!'

We rush around trying to find Mr Enderson, the computer geeky man. We are panicking and tear aggressively into his office like on TV when the police smash into criminals' houses. He is eating pasta bows out of a little plastic Tupperware box and he has taken his shoes off too, showcasing his *Mr Men* socks.

'The power has gone away!' I shout in his face rather rudely, to which he jumps like I've shot a volt of current through his arm, which I straight away feel bad about.

'Oh, not again.' Mr Enderson follows us into the thundery darkness of the computer room and starts poking around some cables and switches . . . I realize that I am holding my breath. I won't have time to rewrite my story . . . I won't be able to be in the magazine . . .

Suddenly the light flickers on and the computers are restarting and I breathe out so much air of relief that my head goes all dizzy.

'Phew, well at least they are back on now,' Mr Enderson says – I can tell he so badly wants to get back to eating them bow ties again, and he deserves to now he has saved my work and my entire career as a journalist. 'From now on, back up all your work onto a hard drive, it will mean that if it happens again you've got everything safe.'

Maggie and I hug and laugh – but then I see the clock. Lunch time is nearly over. I gasp in horror, the football match! *Will!* I said I would be there and I wasn't! I forgot!

'Sorry, Maggie, I've got to . . .' I run out of the computer room and fly down the staircase like I'm in a film trying to find a bomb in a special building or something.

'No running!' shouts Mr Enderson down the stairs behind me and then I think I also hear him groan, 'Nobody ever listens to me.' I've only been at this school a few days and can tell that's true, and so I don't listen either.

I plunge open the big heavy wooden doors and leg it across the tarmac, my shoelaces are undone and the air is freezing, my heart is beating. Guilt filling my throat like sick. I see the boys walking away from the football pitch, and Will's team look defeated but

I can't see Will. I try and look for him through the miserable sweaty tomato faces. No sign of him. And then I see Olly Supperidge, hands on hips, looking horribly smug and proud of himself. He is doing all these showy-off stretches.

'You missed me giving these wimps a good thrashing,' he smirks. I hate the way he speaks and the way he overuses the 'th' in everything – you can almost see his tongue desperately preparing to *spray it not say it.*

'I didn't come to see you, Olly.'

'Which one is your boyfriend then?'

'I don't have or *want* a stupid boyfriend,' I bark back. 'I came to see my best friend.'

'Sorry, Darcy, NO girls play football, not on my watch anyway.' He sniffs. I want to kill him right this second. Kick a football into his head, but to honest, I don't think I can kick a ball and don't want to prove his point accurate. How dare he assume that I could only be friends with girls?

'My best friend IS NOT a girl and also GIRLS CAN play football,' I argue.

'Wrong, and wrong again.' Ollie squirts a bright blue drink into his mouth and lets a few sweat beads dribble down his head like he enjoys it. 'I've never in my life seen a girl who is good at football, only once have I seen a girl play *decent* football and she was the PE teacher from another school and is practically a man anyway so it doesn't count.'

I can't believe how ridiculously small-brained this giant goose boy can be.

'I came to find my best friend, who, yes, happens to be a boy.'

'Boys aren't best friends with girls unless they want to make babies with them, even you must know that.'

'SHUT UP!' I roar, much loader than expected, but I can't help but think about Clementine and Will getting all closey closey these days. Maybe Olly Supperidge is right, perhaps we can't be friends? Perhaps Will does want to make GROSS VILE SICKY babies with Clementine!

'Whoa, calm down, kid!' he laughs, smacking a towel into his face. 'Which one is your (boy) friend?'

He coughs the word (boy) into his towel. I am ready to dissect his belly and drag his guts out onto the pitch for the pigeons to peck on. My face is red and my blood is pulsing.

'I came to see Will. My best friend,' I say each and every word loud and clear.

Olly giggles. 'What, you mean that ginger idiot? He was rubbish. He thought he was SO good last week after that lunch-time hat trick but ha! I injured him in the first ten minutes. Got a yellow card for it, but it was worth it. He was so terrible, it was painful to watch him.'

I am scowling, breathing in and out and in and out and in and out like an engine. I am cross at myself for all my forgetful, neglectful behaviour and yeah, I've messed up, but nobody has annoyed me as much as this. Not all the Clementines or Donald Pinchers or Jamie Haddocks from my old school all mashed together in one. But instead, unexpectedly, tears come.

'You *hurt* him?'

'He's big enough to take care of himself. Don't

be so ridiculous. He had that American girl with him anyway.' I nearly go blind with sadness. I feel like chopping my eyeballs out so I don't have to see this life any more. HOW? WHY? HOW? WHY? Is all that is going through my head. What am I going to do? I turn away and I run, run into the school building as fast as I can. Away from Olly. Quick. Quick. Quick.

'You need to man up, Burdock!' Olly shouts over my head.

Oh, shush the hell up, I am thinking, he does not belong to a boarding school in ancient times where everybody refers to each other by their surnames. *Burdock?* Really. But that *man up* bit has stuck with me like the taste of blood in my mouth. *Man up?* I'll show that Olly how I can 'man up', I'll show him for winding up the world like an oversized jewellery box where the ballerina inside is actually just a wretched decaying zombie. You wait and see.

I pick my pace up and run away from his ratty ghastly face and try to find Will. If he's injured he will be feeling very sorry for himself and no doubt Clementine will be there, dabbing some flannel on his head as though he's Sleeping Beauty and she's the prince. Yeah, that's right, girls can take on the role of the prince too. Sort of. Ish. They can be heroes or whatever. But not Clementine, she is too horrid to be a hero, but oh, SHUT UP, HEAD. I head for the nurse's office, I see his muddy football boots outside the door so I know he is in there. I gently knock on the door.

The nurse bobs her head round the door.

'Hello, Miss Nurse, is Will in there?'

'Afraid so, he has a nasty graze on his face and a few bumps and bruises, but he is OK. Silly boys and their silly football, eh? They will never learn.'

'Can I come in and see him please?' I ask, tears blubbing and bubbling in my eyes. I really didn't feel this same way when we went to visit Cyril in hospital. Not one bit.

'You shouldn't really; it's back to lessons now. Let William rest.'

'*Please*. I am his oldest friend, please let me see him?' I beg her; the words topple out of my mouth like shaken-up lemonade.

'Wait here; let me see if he would like a visitor. What's your name?'

'Darcy, thanks. I mean, my name isn't *Darcy Thanks*, it's just Darcy ... not the *just* bit either, just plain old Darcy.' My brain is all twisted and knotted up.

She smiles all ungenerously and disappears into her little room and shuts the door on me. She better not think I'm his *lover* or anything or else I'll be seriously livid. I just hate all that girlfriend stupid boyfriend business. I wait in the hallway; I look at Will's muddy boots, the blackened laces. This is a terrible year of a life. The nurse pops her head round the doorway again.

'I'm afraid William doesn't want to see anybody right now if that's OK, Darcy? He took quite a bashing today. Maybe give him a ring tonight and see how he is then? His sister Annie is coming to collect him. You should go along to your next lesson now.'

I don't believe her – why on earth would Will not want me, his very best friend in the United World of Everything, to see him? I don't understand.

'Please, can I not just . . . I am sure if I could just see him for one single second I'm sure it would—'

'Darcy, you don't want to get in trouble now, do you? Go on now, lesson time. I'll tell William you sent him your well wishes.'

The nurse smiles shortly again and closes the door. *Well wishes? Well wishes?* He is my friend. And she called him *William*. It's not *William*, it's *Will*. I don't like this stupid nurse and her silly outfit, she doesn't even work in a real-life doctor's with *actual* blood.

I want to cry for ever.

I hate Olly Supperidge too.

So much.

Koala spies me in the hallway at the end of lunch-time rush. She has purple and pink hair mascara on, which is *my* thing. *Who does she think she is?*

'Hey, Darcy.' She spits all over my face but recognizes it this time and wipes her mouth. I can tell by her awkward face and voice that this isn't good news.

'About your story, I've just read it, in the . . . erm . . . computer room with erm Maggie and erm, not to be like rude, but there are some bits in there that I think, I don't know, maybe it's just me, but we're quite . . . I don't think it's right for the magazine—'

I don't even let her finish because the tears are boiling up because I worked hard on that story and I just run up the stairs to history where we are learning about King Henry the Eighth, who is the best king, obviously, but am I enjoying myself? No, not one bit. I am wanting to be with Will to make sure he's all right and that we're still friends. This has been the absolutely worst few weeks of my whole life; it's too much for one person. I HATE OLLY. I HATE MY STORY, IT'S WEIRD AND STUPID. I HATE THE MAGAZINE. I HATE BIGGERER SCHOOL. I am so upset. I don't even know what is happening for the rest of the day as I follow my classmates down the corridors, I am bumping into other kids' shoulders but not feeling a thing, I almost think I could trap my finger in a door right now and I wouldn't notice. I open my day planner and write:

> I had a butterfly in my heart once upon a
> time but now all I have is a coughing
> charcoaled skeleton of a moth.

So dramatical. And then I scribble it out until it just looks like an inky river of blue. Finally, when the bell screams to remind us the day has finished, I pack my books in my bag and that's when I see the slice of pizza wrapped up in the foil, squashed at the very bottom, the pizza that I forgot to eat. I open it up and take it out. The topping has stuck to the top of the foil and the base is all white and soggy and flat. It's a bit stingy on the pepperoni too, Will obviously sneaked a few meaty circles for himself before he wrapped up my slice. I sink my teeth into it and chew and chew and chew. It is like swallowing a car-cleaning sponge, I think, and does not make me feel any better. I trudge to the nurse's room to see if Will is still there but the room is empty.

Wow. I have messed up. Big time.

Chapter Eleven

Once home, everybody knows I am being a weirdo, especially me, but what do I do? I go to pick up the phone and then I remember Will asking me to never call him on the phone again. I don't want to upset him even morer but I can't help myself but to dial his number. I do it really quick so that I don't change my mind.

Annie answers.

'Hello, Annie, it's me, Darcy.'

'Oh hi, Darcy?' Annie sounds awkward, like she was warned not to answer the phone to me a bit, I can really tell.

'Is Will there?' I ask.

'Errrm . . . let me just go check.'

Who has to *errrrrrrm let me just go check* to know if somebody is home or not, it's not like they live in a gigantic palace with fourteen hundred and a zillion bedrooms where people can come and go without anybody noticing.

Annie lifts up the phone again. 'Hi, Darcy. Will . . . William doesn't really feel like speaking right now, he has a headache . . .'

William? *William?*

'Please let me speak to him, Annie.'

'I want to, Darcy, but he . . . William . . . doesn't want to . . . I'm sorry.'

'Annie, please?'

'Hold on,' she says, and then I hear her murmuring mixed in with the TV followed by Will's whispers.

'Yeah?' It's him.

'Will!' I say brightly.

'It's William now,' he bites back.

'OK.' *Ouch ouch ouch.* 'I didn't know, you didn't tell me you changed your name.'

'Yeah, well . . . I actually didn't change it, that is my real name.' His words cut me up like squashed fruit in a blender.

'How are you feeling?' I ask, trying to sound light and breezy.

'Like rubbish.'

'I heard what happened, I came to the nurse's office but she wouldn't let me see you.'

'Yeah. I heard you outside.'

This was horrible. *Really* horrible.

'I'm really sorry I didn't make it to see you play football.'

'You know what, Darcy, since you've started wearing your hair in that plait you've become a new different person, one that I just don't like. I always am there for you, and when I ask you to be there for me, the one time, you're not . . . I don't want to be your friend, not now, not today, not tomorrow, not with that brushed hair.'

It's the most words Will . . . *iam* ever said in one go and they are the worserest words I've ever heard.

They don't sink in. I am not upset just yet; I am mainly really very shocked. He hangs up the phone and I grip onto Lamb-Beth. The hang-up beep noise is ringing in my ear; so *final* like the machines in hospitals on TV that beep when somebody's heart has stopped beating.

At the table, Poppy's going on and on and on and on about some stupid new friend she's made at her stupid dance lesson who's a boy and she's all excited but it's making me madderer and sadderer. I don't eat hardly any of the curry Dad has made. I just eat a few blobs of rice and then head upstairs and open up my writing book. My lungs are squashing under the guilt and sadness.

Sorry is a word that aches our mouths, that hurts our teeth and scratches our tongue. Sometimes it's craved for like a hot milk or a bath or a favourite song on the radio, a hand hold from somebody that cares. Sometimes it's oversaid and overdone and as normal as taking a shower. Other times it smothers you completely, it falls in the eyes and the nostrils, chokes the throat like swallowing a rag, clogging up the earholes and bruising everything it can in its warpath. It can be known to be patient, timed perfectly, folded away into a brown envelope. Others are spring-action *sorrys*, meticulously technified, hinged and perfectly constructed with timed spines like the beauty of a pop-up book. Some are sloppy and unexpected, pour out of the messy mouth like a swear word or a regret. Some are 'Cry wolf's, shamelessly singing the words and sounds to their own apologies like memories from childhood that are too sweet and too fatty. A chubby sorry.

> Sometimes a sorry is a boomerang and hits you back on the head in a good way or more often in a bad way. Sometimes you get a sorry back.

When I finish writing a spider crawls out of my hair and lands on my hand. *Oh, hi so much, spider.* It feels good to see a creature in my groomed flat straight nest. Maybe Will's right, maybe the hairbrush is tidying all my Darcy-ness away?

I hate this brushed hair, it isn't who I am or who I am wanting to be either. I'm never doing it again. Ever.

After putting the spider on the windowsill I take my hairbrush and I start scuffing it up again and making it deliberately morer and morer knotty, and it's not working and I am getting so crosserer and fed up with this straight and normal hair that I just take my scissors and chop my hair off.

Just. Like. That.

I look in the mirror. It looks bad. Lamb-Beth looks at me, like 'Oh dear'. She can shut up. But it does look really so bad. So bad and not one bit nice. It looks all wonky and disastrous, like a big animal has eaten a chunk of it out. Oh no. I am mad. I am crazy. I can't be upset or else I'll get in trouble. I have to stand by this. I find Mum's hair mousse and I fizz a big dollop of it into my hand like a giant mash potato bun of marshmallow, and it smells of chocolate and vanilla and then I flop it into the bad haircut.

I run down to my mum who is plucking her eyebrows on the couch and is talking to the TV like it's a politician she doesn't agree with. Dad has got his feet in the washing-up bowl filled up with hot bubbly water but his feet are a bit too big for this makeshift foot bath and the water is splodging and spilling out and also I wish he wouldn't give his feet a jacuzzi in the same place we wash up our knives and forks.

'Mum, Dad, I cut my hair,' I announce, attention-seeking, naturally.

'Cool,' says Dad, his eyes flickering   he's always enjoyed my rebellious streak because he has a couple of tattoos and back in the day he wore leather jackets.

'Fruit loop,' says Mum, but that's before she can tear her eyes away from the TV, and once she looks up she screams, 'Darcy! What have you DONE?' and I burst into tears about my whole entire life.

'I can't take it,' I dribble through the tears.

'Take what, love?' Mum hugs me close; her eyebrow hairs float onto my hand like hairy tears from her eyes. Dad turns the TV down and comes and sits next to me. I am smudged in the middle of

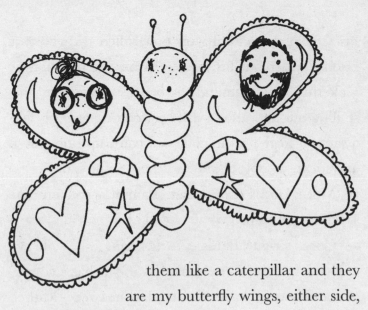

them like a caterpillar and they
are my butterfly wings, either side,
really wanting me to fly.

'Any of it.' I put my head into my hands and think
about how to explain. Dad does a clicky thing with
his mouth that invites Lamb-Beth immediately into
the living room and she bundles in straight away and
up onto my lap.

'Go on, monkey, tell us . . .' Mum says. 'I can
guarantee you that everything you're feeling, one of
us will have felt the same before.'

So I start from the top, about Will and Clementine

and the story and Olly and how Koala said my story was rubbish – well, she didn't exactly *say* that but she didn't have to, I knew what she was thinking.

I sometimes can't take the fact that mums and dads just *have to love you*. Sometimes I can be so difficult to love. I know not all kids get that. Some kids get no love shared out to them at all, but if you are one that's loved it's probably a good idea to drink it up a bit. Mum's right, I am a fruit loop.

Chapter Twelve

'What happened to your hair?' Poppy says over breakfast.

'What happened to your general whole whatever the hell on earth you are?' I stutter back, embarrassed. I get up and throw my cereal into the sink to make an impact. Annoying. I wanted to eat that.

'Darcy had a little experiment with the scissors, didn't you, chick?' Mum smiles. She helped me even the other side of my hair out a bit last night so that I don't look so completely mental, and I think our chat on the sofa has made me feel a little lighter . . . although maybe that's just from being now a bit bald.

'Well, anyway, Timothy is coming over to our house tonight for dinosaur chicken and chips and letter-shaped pasta.' Poppy sips her juice; she still holds it with two hands like an absolute animal creature child.

'Who's Timothy?'

'My new friend that's a boy as well even.' Show-off.

'Is he imaginary?'

'No, of course he is *not*, and you're horrible.' Poppy looks hurt.

I do an inside sigh. I've upset her now. Mum looks crossly at me. Poppy has wanted a friend that's a boy ever since Will and I became friends. I am being nasty ruining it for her.

'Sorry, Poppy, I was joking, I didn't mean it. I can't wait to meet Timothy.'

'Good, you better run home from school so you can meet him because I told him you were cool.'

'You told him I was cool . . . well, why did you do that?'

'Well 'cos you are, aren't you?'

It's Friday. Thank goodness, I think, as I walk up to the school gates, I could do with two days away from this wretched place. I find Maggie the moment I go into the building. She looks all relieved and excited because the magazine is 'put to bed' (this is what you do to magazines, I am such a professional journalist) but I am about to crash and wreck all that for her.

'Nice hair,' she says, grinning. I don't have the time to work out if she's being sarcastic or not as this is clearly an emergent . . . or is it an urgent? Oh, not now.

'I want to try and write another story for the magazine,' I rush out.

'What?' She looks like she's about to collapse. 'Darcy, you

can't, the magazine's deadline was yesterday – *remember* the crazy mayhem in the computer room, that wasn't for a joke, you know? You can't do that.'

'I have to.'

'Darcy, I'm sorry, you just don't have time.'

'I have to. *Please?*'

Maggie bites her lip and scrunches her face up. 'I don't understand, it's not something Olly said, was it? Ignore him, he's a fool.'

'No, no, it's not to do with him . . . I want to, *have* to put a special story in.'

'Can't it go in the next issue?'

I really notice I am sounding horribly spoiled and stubborn and ridiculous to think I could put the whole magazine at risk but I just need to fix things. I hang my head. This isn't going to go down well with the others. Gosh, I feel crazy with this ugly hair and bonkers head. Maggie looks pale.

'Lunch time. Meet me in the computer room. Don't be late,' Maggie breathes out and closes her eyes. 'Now get out of my sight.' She squeezes out a smile showing me she's not cross in real life too much and then rushes away not looking at me once.

The whole morning is spent scribbling and thinking and speed writing as quick I can. I get in trouble only once by Mr Hatfield in science because he thought I wasn't concentrating (which I wasn't, actually) but the limelight soon swam off me when Ellie Richards got told off for making everybody laugh by pretending two magnets were doing snogging and then Marcus Wilde took it one step further by eating a mouthful of iron filings. People will do *anything* to get a laugh. I meet Maggie at lunch time, as promised, with my finished story. I hand it to her, out of breath. Koala walks past me and doesn't smile. I've annoyed her, I can tell. I really am a troublemakerer.

'Don't worry about her,' Maggie tuts and lets me hand the story over. 'We're just stressing. I'm sure your story is worth the wait.'

'Yeah, right!' I hear Olly's gurgle from across the room, twirling round on his stupid seat, shaking his head. 'Nice work, Burdock . . . *not*!' He snarls and pretends to flick through a book he's reading.

Maggie opens the first page of text. 'Darcy,' she whispers privately as quietly as she can to not embarrass me, 'mate, this isn't typed up.' She grits her teeth.

'I know, I didn't have time,' I apologize.

'We can't, Darcy; the magazine is going to print, on a file, how can we sort this now? It will take ages to type up and—'

It's too late, Koala stomps over, and I've never seen her so *irritated*, her fringe is almost standing on end.

'Let me see!' she spits and scans my pathetic sprawl. 'It's full of mistakes and errors too, Darcy, we can't publish this. It will let the editorial team down.'

Olly begins to laugh and does lots of cartoon pretend-crying like the clowns do at the circus followed by lots of upside-down thumbs. I want to slash his head off.

Suddenly Maggie, Queen Saviour, pipes up:

'Hold on . . . we can scan it. As it is. Scan it in, save it as PDF, drop it in. It will take two seconds. It's Darcy's story, so Darcy's choice. We support our writers. We should let her publish it. As it is. Not everything needs to be polished: this is real.'

There is an empty minute where nobody quite knows what to do. Everybody looks at Koala, my insides are jumping. She flashes me a brief eye glance, her eyelashes patter, angered.

'Oh— Be quick about it.'

'What? You've got to be joking me? I can't believe this is happening?' Olly is screeching at the top of his voice, getting more and more high-pitched. Koala gets up and walks out and then Olly leaps after her, shouting, 'Koala, Koala bear!'

Bit affectionate, if you ask me, but that's not for now. I want to squeal I am so excited, but there is no time for that either and I don't want to annoy anybody even more than I already have. But seriously, *phew*.

* * *

I finally see Will at the end of the day but he doesn't
see me or at least pretends not to. I can only watch
from afar as he is surrounded by a wall of boys that
seem to know he is the best thing ever mixed with a
tired hero as he shows them his bumps and bruises.
Tomorrow is Clementine's birthday so no doubt she
will fit snug into my best friend's shoes and I'll be
forgotten. Fine. I just want to go home and wrap
myself up in Lamb-Beth and be as tiny as the garlic
that comes out from the garlic crusher and let myself
have one more day of feeling sorry for myself before
I can get back to being an excellent thing.

But so much for that! When I get home I can hear

all this boshing and stomping around upstairs, and a wild shrilling scream is coming from Poppy's room. Mum looks like she's about to crack up and then I remember . . . Timothy.

'You have *got* to meet Timothy,' she smirks.

I pretend I'm not excited, pick up Lamb-Beth for a cuddle and go to eat a Dairylea triangle. It's certainly one of those snacks that I prefer unwrapping than eating, unlike chocolates.

'Darcy's home!' Mum calls up the stairs and winks at me. Hector is eating a few books on the floor; he has been eating pages for ages these days.

A sudden rumble pours down the stairs. Poppy is wearing her ballerina tutu. She is all excited. 'Darcy, you're home, and it's *Friday*!' she announces as though she's *made* Friday. As though Friday was her idea. And then she says, 'Darcy, meet Timothy.'

I see a ballet shoe land on the top stair, then the next stair and then the next, perfectly timed, accurately placed, as delicate as a cat. Timothy's skin is the colour of caramel, his eyes are hazel, his hair is curled and gelled, his features are exact and dramatic. His gaze is focused on Poppy and he is in FULL pink tutu himself, tights and all. When he reaches the last landing he curtseys, beautifully, and then bows.

'Well, when I saw this tutu I thought, *Get me in that* immmmediately.' He laughs a tiny tinny cackle. 'You must be Darcy, I've heard *so* much about you.' He throws his arms into the air.

I laugh. 'Really nice to meet you, Timothy.' I go to shake his hand because I have never really felt this *introduced to* anybody before, but Timothy doesn't really want me to do any of that. He pulls me in close and kisses the air either side of my

face four times, making an over-dramatic 'M-WAH, M-WAH, M-WAH' sound, just like we are American girls going shopping on TV. Mum hides her face in her jumper to stop herself from laughing. Timothy is her new favourite, I can tell.

'I love your hair, babes, it's so *rocky*.' Is this boy really in Poppy's dance class? She's so lucky. 'Poppy, let's get your mum to make us a glass of fizzy pop and then let's play Barbies. Darcy, do you want to play *Ken*?'

'What do you mean, *play Ken*?' I ask. My eyebrows are confused but I really like this Timothy.

Timothy sneaks a smirk and then begins. 'OK, well, it's a long story but Poppy's character, Bianca (to be pronounced kinda French like Bea-yunk-ha) is like the nicest girl in the world, I mean like Taylor Swift nice, blonde hair, blue eyes, works as a vet, I mean wouldn't hurt a fly, total babe. Now she's been dating Ken for like *ever*. My character, Brittney-Charlotte Mariah Holmes, is Bianca's long-lost sister; she has come back, for good. She's like a total meanie, I mean like *major*, but she's also mega fierce and hot and all the guys like totally fancy her, so she steals Ken off Bianca, things are about to heat up in the face-off between the love triangle, gonna be tragic, up for it?' Poppy screws her face up; she is worrying this isn't going to work out between Timothy and me.

'So let me get this straight, you know how you said that Brittney-Charlotte Mariah Holmes *stole* Ken off

Bianca?' I ask, trying to work this out in my head.

Timothy nods.

'Did Ken have a choice in this?'

'Duh, like Brittney-Charlotte Mariah Holmes is like mega hot, like spicy.'

'So maybe it's time for Bianca to steal something off *Brittney*?' I am plot-thickening, obviously.

'Well . . . it's kinda *not* in Bianca's nature to do that,' Poppy dives in.

'Yeah, well maybe Bianca just hasn't met Leslie Rachel yet?' My eyes twinkle. Leslie Rachel, my one and only Barbie that lies waiting patiently under my bed in a swimming costume and glittery leggings, Leslie Rachel with the pink and purple dip dye and the flaming fire in her eyes. She has been waiting for this moment for ever. 'Timothy . . . *let's play Barbies.*'

Hours later when the doorbell rings we just *know* it's Timothy's mum come to collect him. This bliss couldn't go on for the rest of lives, but we are sad. Timothy is the world's best fun. Watching him play with a doll dressed as a ballerina fairy was just very

. . . I can't think of the exact wording . . . but good. It was really good. We roll reluctantly down the stairs. Timothy's mum has beautiful long make-you-jealous dreadlocks and loads of wooden jewellery on. She has a big silver nose piercing and long red nails and a happy face.

'Bet you loved it here, eh, Tim? These girls look like fun!' she beams.

'They'll do, I suppose,' Timothy jokes and gets his fur coat from off the banister. We all giggle.

'He's so cheeky. That coat was mine, you know,' his mum says. 'From the eighties. His older sister didn't want it, it's not real fur or nothing, but it was expensive. Never did I imagine Timothy would want to wear it.' She laughs. 'Thing is though, he looks better than any of us would.' And we all laugh at that because it's true.

We say goodnights and then we close the door. Poppy looks so proud she could burst. She found a good one, she really did. Mum puts the TV on and we all pile up for a bit of *The Simpsons* before Mum's boring real-life TV show starts.

Dad comes home from work smelling like a sawdusty hamster – his job is working with wood so sometimes he smells all pet-like. He has to go on a work trip tomorrow so he doesn't want to watch TV with us. He's going to FRANCE!!! Even on a SATURDAY!! And I can tell he's mostly really being in a bad mood because of this. Even though he has to go, he doesn't like being away from us lot one bit. It's that weird thing people do when they ruin the time they have with their families by moaning about the times they have to go away. It's silly. But

I understand, I hate saying goodbye to my dad. He kicks his shoes off all grumpy.

'You and your bloody soap operas,' Dad tuts, making Mum go *Shhhh, shhhhh, shhhhh* and try to listen in closer to the TV. I'm just sooo jealous thinking about all the baguette Dad's going to get to eat.

'What's a soap opera, Mum?' I ask her, but her eyes are all squinty. I hate soap. The way it slides and glides out of your grasp when you are trying to make it stay still for just simply one moment. New soap is just as annoying because when you immediately see it all you want to do is dig your nails into it one billion times but you are not allowed to, otherwise Mum goes, 'Now that's silly, isn't it?'

Have you ever been to the opera? It's where people all go with massive mouths and giant frowns and sing words but really draaaaaag them out for an ever. Just like Henrietta from next door. That was her job before she retired and just started her career as being nosy. So what is a Soap Opera? I have heard this word a couple of times and I just cannot imagine for my mind what on earth this is at all. I bet you are thinking of singing soap. I do hope so.

Dad's all of a sudden laughing to himself, sniggering like he is a fat hen sitting on a secret story egg. He seems to have cheered up,

'What are you laughing at?' Mum asks him, as they cuddle a bit.

'Nothing.' He grins.

'You might be able to lie to your customers but you cannot lie to your wife, what are you laughing at?'

'My new game,' he chokes.

'What game?' Mum smile-frowns.

'It's a silly thing,' Dad says.

'Well, you're a silly man.'

'OK, when I drive, in the car, on my own, sometimes . . . I wave at people.'

'To who?'

'Everybody.'

'Why?'

'To see who waves back.'

'But why?'

'Why not?'

'And do people wave back?'

'Not usually, but that's why I'm laughing now.'

'Oh?'

'Because today somebody waved me back and I was so excited, I thought, finally, as human beings we can actually say *hello* to each other and then I looked up and I realized it was Henrietta from next door walking her dog.'

We all laugh and so does he. And then Mum turns to Dad with a Mask of Seriousness on and says, 'Do me a favour, love? Stop waving at strangers, it's odd and the neighbours will talk.'

Poor only-trying-to-be-nice Dad.

Before bed I don't know why but I suddenly really don't want Dad to go away tomorrow, even though he goes away all the time I just can't imagine him not being there for when I wake up. I should be used to it by now and know exactly how to act but I feel lonesome. I sit on his lap and curl into a ball to try and be tiny, even smaller than Hector, and bunch my whole body up and I want to say 'Don't go.' But Mum says we are not allowed to say that to Dad when he has to go away because it makes it more hard for him. Why am I being such a delicate fragile baby child? I just want to stay there and let Dad wrap his arms all tight around me and I hear him breathe me in. I feel a blob of little water touch my shoulder and I secretly taste it and it tastes like tear but I would never ask if it was tear because he's a dad and I don't want him to never not feel like a lion.

Chapter Thirteen

Saturday morning, yawn-o'-clock, and just like last week I have more homework than I had in my whole life at my old school pushed together. I physically couldn't even get any more homework, like it actually properly isn't possible, unless they want me to wind up being flattened like a pancake under a giant heap of home-work paper like the hoarder people you see on TV that can't throw anything away. I won't be able to make my 100th birthday party because I'll just be too busy 'finishing this bit of homework'. I bet Will is looking forward to stupid Clementine's birthday. I can't even believe that he would even contemplate going to that horror banquet. Some people never fail to immensely depress me. Playing Barbies with Poppy and Timothy was refreshing because it took the worries off my back for a bit and made me feel young and caring free-ish. I try to think abut that and not to care that Will still hasn't tried to speak to me once. A cuddle with my sheep always helps . . .

LAMB-BETH. Where is she? She usually appears in my room for a snuggle as soon as I wake up . . .

I look under the bed – no Lamb-Beth.

I look behind my bookcase – no Lamb-Beth.

I look on top of my washing pile – no Lamb-Beth.

NOT . . .

In the bathroom

In the bath

In the sink

In Poppy's bedroom

On her bed

On her desk

In her bin

In Hector's room

In his toy box

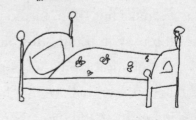

Not hidden in with his pants and socks

Not in Mum and Dad's room

Not on the staircase

Not in the garage because we don't actually have one

Not in the living room

Not in the kitchen

Not in the toaster

Not rolled up under the oven

Not behind the curtains silently sleeping

Not on the sofa

Not behind the TV

Not hidden in the magazines

Not rolled up in my mittens

And then it hit me like a rock . . .

Lamb-Beth has gone missing!

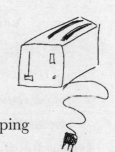

Chapter Fourteen

Drip drip drip drip went the kitchen tap. *Tick tick tick tick* went the living-room clock. *Sob sob sob sob* went Poppy. But the only noise I could hear was empty. It was official: Lamb-Beth was gone. Grandma arrived just in time for the drama. Just having my grandma with me made me feel a bit safer.

Mum went driving around in the car looking for Lamb-Beth with our family circumstance friend, Marnie Pincher, and we waited indoors, feeling helpless and worried. Her posh snobby son Donald Pincher walked around with his hands in his pockets trying to recite as many jokes as he could remember to cheer us up, but it was just sounding annoying so I told him to shut up and he started to tuck into the crisps drawer. He better not eat all the beef ones or else we will be coming to blows. I keep thinking *Haven't you got SOMETHING to do on a Saturday?* about Donald but stop myself from being mean, it's not his fault he annoys everybody and so has to be best friends with his mum.

We sat with Grandma as the reality of a lost Lamb-Beth crept on like an invisibility cloak and made everything harder to see and made things feel sadder and weirder and colder and only made Lamb-Beth more losterer.

I keep feeling tears swamping over my eyes like sinking stones; washed away. I kept trying to be strong as I concentrated on counting the wrinkle lines on Grandma's hand as it held mine. The sleepy whimpers of a TV programme that Grandma liked churning in the background. I want to not be alive a bit.

Dad kept calling from his work trip in France for news and he kept asking to speak to me but I had nothing to say except for *ouch ouch ouch ouch ouch ouch* as my heart was hurting so much. Mum kept telling me to call Will, but I didn't want to speak to him because I didn't know what to say, but Mum was saying I was only letting Lamb-Beth down by not as we needed as many eyes as we could out searching for her. I picked up the phone but put it down again instantly. I couldn't do it. Anyway, he was probably getting ready for Clementine's *really posh restaurant* and *really gross boring party*. But Mum was right, we had to get a search party together to comb the London streets, and if anybody knew those London streets it was my greatest enemy of all time, from small school, even worser than Olly and

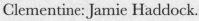

Clementine: Jamie Haddock.

I found him, as always, by the sweet shop, picking bits of wall out of a stranger's front drive and he actually looked *happy* to see me. I explained that it was 'purely business' and 'didn't mean we were friends' but 'I would appreciate his help', and to all of that he said 'Whatever I can do to help.' Which I wasn't expecting, considering he was my all-time enemy. Jamie was at the really rough boys' school for all the hideously naughty bad boys that the world could collect. They all got scooped up and thrown in there like poisonous spiders, even though Jamie Haddock wasn't nearly as bad as what everybody thought. Plus he had a bike, so could travel far and wide to find my Lamb-Beth.

Jamie suggested writing down all the things that Lamb-Beth loved, to try and work out where she might be.

Water
Ripping things up
Chewing Dad's shirts
Food
Flowers
Blankets
Chocolate buttons
Curtains
Me

I started to cry. Tears are sneaky, they are so rude, and they just turn up always uninvited. Gate-crashing everything. I had no control of my eyes or my brain. It was like I was a boily egg and somebody had just whacked a huge teaspoon over my head and split my shell-mind into plenty of bits and

pieces and egg brain was going everywhere. Jamie kept his eyes on the denim of his jeans, which judging by how red my face was was probably the best place for them.

'We will find her,' he whispered and pulled out some overheated jelly snakes from his pocket that had turned to hairy goo, and offered me one. He then began to shake a bit from nervousness and mumbled something about going to look for Lamb-Beth and then decided to pedal away on his bike really quickly. I feel so touched and happy that he's helping me to find her, maybe he isn't such a rotten egg after all?

After the whole day of being scared and worried I was exhausted and Mum said we had to relax now or else we wouldn't sleep and be able to carry on searching the next day either. I had so much trapped up stuff inside and without any Will to explode with I had to write something down.

You Are More Than A Lamb To Me

Each moment that we are together
Makes me float like I am a feather
When I look up it's your eyes I see
You are more than a lamb to me.

Every morning when I wake up and see you
I feel noodles in my oodles, I'm so happy
   I know you
You make each day so light and easy
You are more than a lamb to me.

I know what spins around your precious
   head
As you snore at the other end of the bed
You are so warm and kind and friendly
You are more than a lamb to me.

I sniff your smell to remind myself
That I couldn't possibly love another else

Your little soul grumbling next to mine sweetly
You are more than a lamb to me.

Out in the cold wet night all alone
Brings nonsense and worry to my bones
When will you come home to me?
You are more than a lamb to me.

And as I try to be asleep tonight
I dream of you snuggling tight
Nuzzling my face reminding me too
That I am more than a Darcy to you.

Mum comes home with Marnie Pincher all empty-handed and sad and Marnie keeps saying 'We looked everywhere' but I don't believe them. Grandma has made a big pot of pea and ham soup, which everybody starts slurping and burning the roofs of their mouths on, but I don't feel like eating.

And actually, even if I did decide to burn the roof of my mouth I know I wouldn't be even able to feel a single one thing because I am *that* sad.

I start to get angry at Will too and slip from tears to rage to tears to rage back to tears again. Even though nothing is his fault he should be here but instead he's probably at a burger bar or rib shack or watching *High School Musical* with Clementine before going off to her horriblest yuckiest party that was obviously designed by evil horror dream cooker-uppers. It feels like he is on the other side of the moon, so far away, shaking hands with the human form of HATE. It's like I don't even know him. I try not to think about it but the idea of him laughing and joking and giving Clementine her present is enough to make me cry or punch a wall. I am full blown utterly sick with jealousy about this. I close my eyes to try and block out the reality and listen to the silence.

Nothing.

Dad's getting the firstest train back that he can, which will make things a bit better – really can't wait

to see him and our family puzzle to be put a bit more together.

Mum says Timothy (brilliant) and Donald (hmmm) can sleep over, which is betterer than being all by myself. So we all set up a massive duvet den in the living room to make it cosy and warm and Marnie decides to stay over too 'to keep an eye' on us so Mum and Grandma can have some rest. It's funny how situations cause everyday life to get all upside-down and back to front. All we need is Lamb-Beth to come home to put things right again.

We watch a few cartoons and have some hot chocolate but I keep falling in and out of sadness so much like I have a split personality and it's one by one when everybody gently eventually starts snoring off to sleep that I panic and I think, *I'm never going to see my Lamb-Beth ever again.*

I can't stop thinking about her quivering wet rain-soaked coat, her soggy eyelashes, her shivering little feet, her lost mind. Eventually I fall asleep by the soft poundings of my own heart.

The next day is hollow hell. Like, OUCH! No word from anybody about our lamb and it's Sunday so I really should be enjoying myself on this 'not being in school day', planning my world domination or doing something *fun*, not worrying. But I can't relax because we've still heard *nothing*. No news.

Dad comes home from France early, which proves

he must love Lamb-Beth huge amounts of a lot. He has tired eyes and is carrying a stack of paper and pens and some photocopied pictures of Lamb-Beth to make missing signs and we pin them all the way up the road on every lamppost and in the window of the vets and in the windows of some of the shops.

We come home and the house feels very dry and cold like the soil of a dead plant.

'Oh, monkey.' Mum kisses me; it sounds the same as when a new pot of jam is opened.

Have you ever lost something you love? Well, it hurts like mad.

Grandma sticks around for a bit more time which is nice and so we try to do normalish things later on, like going to Pizza Express which is a quite normal thing to do as a treat but it isn't treat or celebration time, is it? No. In fact, quite the opposite and coming into Pizza Express with their marbly tables and men rolling out dough in stripy T-shirts is making me fall on the wrong side of cross. Still, I have to eat, I guess. Each swallow hurts.

And then *this* happens . . .

DAD   I spoke to Marnie (Pincher) today. She says
      that the house next-door-but-one's dog has had
      puppies. I thought that, perhaps, if everybody
      wanted to, we could perhaps, maybe, go and
      take a look at them.

POPPY   Hooray! Timothy has a pug dog so –
      Yes yes yes, please, oh, I love dogs and mostly
      puppies, oh hooray, can we go now, now, now?
      I'll eat all my pizza down in one go or we can
      put it in a takeaway
      box, oh yes, oh yes, oh
      yes.

      HECTOR   Oh,
      I would LOVE a
      dog. Let's call him
      Monster.

      MUM   A dog? That's
      a good idea.

Then everybody looks at me and my knife and fork are rattling on the table in rage, my pizza has trans-formed into a pit of burning fire. My eyebrows dip, my teeth grit, Angrosaurus rex is coming out of me, my blood is boiling. Grandma orders herself a large brandy.

ME   Why on EARTH would we WANT to look at some STUPID PUPPIES when LAMB-BETH is missing?

MUM   I don't think Dad meant it like that, Darcy, I think he was just trying to be helpful.

ME   Helpful? How?

POPPY   By getting us something new to love, of course.

ME   NEW TO LOVE? *NEW TO LOVE? Have you lost your mind?*

DAD   Come on, monkey, I didn't me—

ME   Don't *monkey* me.

DAD   I honestly didn't mean it like that, we could never replace Lamb-Beth, she's part of the family.

Then Poppy starts to cry because she misses Lamb-Beth and then so does Hector and for maybe 0.5 seconds I sort of see why we were talking about getting a puppy because there was a hole in our world without Lamb-Beth. But the hole was Lamb-Beth-shaped. Grandma sips her brandy and pretends to flick through her little diary even though the only plans in there are probably reading her book and making soup.

We get up and leave Pizza Express after paying our bill and a new family sit down in our seats as quick as can be and this annoys me so much. When you eat at a restaurant you begin to feel like that table is yours – it's a horrible sight to see new people in your chair acting out your lifestyle. It's like watching intruders plod around your kitchen using your whisk or whatever.

She can't just have *gone*. Colds *go*. Tempers *go*. Lambs don't go! I can't digest it at all. I wish she would come back to me.

Chapter Fifteen

Monday, the launch of the magazine, and the day has not started ideally. No Lamb-Beth and no Will being my friend really puts the sourest of tastes in my mouth and I didn't sleep at all well. We're up early as Grandma wakes up at hours that don't even exist they are so early and Dad makes us peanut butter on toast and sweet tea because it's still so freezing outside and we need warming up. I don't like Mondays. Or Tuesdays or Wednesdays, and actually Thursdays or Fridays or Saturdays or not even Sundays. In fact, Sunday is my worserest of all because it tricks you like it's a free empty play day but really you spend all of Sunday dreading Monday, which was never as bad as what Sunday decided to pretend it was. Sunday, the hammy drama king.

As we had cried quite a lot over missing Lamb-Beth we have red giant panda stains around our eyes that actually made Mum laugh a bit, as those red rings with my terrible new hair do . . . (or hair *don't*) make me look like a Victorian ghost, which would be perfect for Halloween which was just round the corner but would come and go unnoticed and uncelebrated if Lamb-Beth didn't come home and Will decided to still enjoy hating me. We thought we maybe shouldn't go to school today but Grandma said school might distract us and help us *get on with it*, that we'd be no use *moping around crying* or *feeling sorry for ourselves*.

Life must go on, Grandma says as we leave our housy comfort behind for another day of empty no-Will-friendship, pressure from the school magazine about my risky gamble of putting a new handwritten spelling-mistooked story in, which will mean Mrs Ixy is going to be disappointed in me and then triple trouble for me not doing my homework over the weekend due to trauma. Not forgetting all of that . . . the worserest bit of all – NO Lamb-Beth to hug onto. I lean my head against the car window and watch the world slip by outside.

On the way, after dropping off Poppy and Hector, we sit in morning traffic and I see a huge derelict building, gutted and empty, the windows all smashed in and the insides showing themselves off like it's in the middle of an operation. I look closer; I can just make out the design of leftover wallpaper of a bedroom, tiles from the bathroom. I see the edges of a picture frame even, some battered books on the bookshelf.

'Sad,' Mum sighs to herself. 'That was a beautiful

house once, but they had a fire.'

'A *fire*?' My eyes widen. It's hard to imagine all those chaotic bright orange flames ripping everything up now it's so dull and grey and concrete.

'It was in the paper,' Mum continued, watching the road carefully. 'The family are fine, but *everything* they loved was in that house, their memories, their history. Just look at it now.'

I gulp and look harder, and it all becomes clear: the black smoke and charcoal burns on the wall, the decaying crumbling brick, the sprays of dirt dust splattered on every edge of the house. I see the houses next to it, mirroring what this house once was, reminding it every day that it was once as elegant and as amazing as them. We pull away just after I notice a tiny bluebell flower shooting through the heap of ashes. A little shade of hope.

I put things into (big word alert) *perspective*, like how I'm meant to do this days and I'm groaned up.

218

All this moaning I've been doing, all this crying and stomping and arguing and complaining when some people have to deal with things like *this*. I am embarrassed and ashamed. I will change my attitude. Lamb-Beth will come back. Will and I WILL work it out, the magazine will be successful and homework, well . . . it's just homework, it's not the end of the world.

We reach my school gates, I slam the car door shut and I roll out, head high, into the world, one foot after the other, one foot after the other, one foot after the other, one foot after the other . . .

And that was when I saw *everybody* stood around reading the school magazine. Clementine leaning against the wall with her all upturned sourpuss face (like an unhappy cat) and scoffing.

'I can't go in.' I shake my head to Mum.

'What?' she yaps abruptly. 'Stop being so over-dramatic and get into school, you will be late.'

'No, Mum, I *can't*.' I look at her with my hugest saucer-like eyes.

'But I've got a client.' (Mum is one of those

creative types that does roughly one hundred jobs: at the moment she is cutting and bleaching women's hair in our bathroom when we're at school.) She narrows her eyes into two darts. 'Darcy, you can't just *not* go to school because you don't feel like it, imagine if I didn't get up to take you to school in the morning because I didn't *feel* like it – you'd never get to school. *EVER.*'

'Good. Well, you should listen to your *feelings* more often then, that would be fine by me,' I joke, pushing the line a bit, but it makes Mum crack a naughty smile and she takes a breath in and looks at the intensity bubbling around the school gates and probably remembers what it was like in her schooldays and how scary everything was. She sees everybody reading the magazine too, but she doesn't say anything about that being the reason for my freakout, Mum's good like that. She looks back at me. Then there is this brief moment between us.

'We will tell them about Lamb-Beth going missing. Everyone will be kind to you all day then.'

'I don't want to tell them about Lamb-Beth,' I say.

'Why not?' she asks.

'In case she doesn't come home and then everybody asks me about her every day,' I whisper, and I feel those pesky tears start to prick my eyeballs again.

Mum accepts this information immediately. 'OK. You will have to say you felt sick. I can get in trouble for keeping you out of school like this.'

'Of course.' I nod quickly.

'And Grandma, she's very strict about these things and I don't want her thinking her son has married a mad woman.'

I scrinch my face up because if it's one thing Grandma *knows* it's that Dad has married a mad woman. I decide to keep this truth to myself.

'I'm serious, Darcy. I mean, this is the sort of naughtiness mums go to prison for.' *All right*, I'm thinking, *don't milk it*. I get back into the car and we drive away from school, just this once.

BBBBBBBBBBBBBBBBRRRRRRRINNNNNG
BBBBBBBBBBBBBBBBRRRRRRRINNNNNG
BBBBBBBBBBBBBBBBRRRRRRRINNNNNG

The phone is screaming the moment we get home. Grandma has fallen to sleep on the sofa so Mum runs for it, lifting the phone out of the cradle and whispers a 'hello'. She then looks at me, first confused and untrusting and then her eyes popping out of her round glasses. 'Darcy!' she yells, startling Grandma. 'Darcy, it's good news!'

After cancelling Mum's 'client' (if you can call the loony housewife from round the corner who is looking for a therapist more than a hairstylist a client) Mum and me get in the car and drive for what seems like a squillion years. You know when a place is roughly a squillion miles away because you have to stop off for petrol on the way. I like the way petrol smells, but there is no time for that now.

We drive into this big green field full of plants and vegetables and fruit and sheds and scarecrows. I hate scarecrows, with their horrid hay faces and scruffy zombic clothing. This place, Mum says, is called an 'allotment' and it's a shared garden space where people can grow their own food instead of getting it from the supermarket.

The lady from the phone call, Mandy, trudges over to the car with a very much pleased-with-herself smile. She is wearing one of those sleeping bag jackets with the arms chopped off – she still had her actual arms though, phew. Her breath shows in the cold air like she is a fire-breathing dragon, but a nice one obviously. Gosh, I really do like dragons and I don't think about them enough.

'You must be Mollie?' She grins, and Mum nods.

On the walk through the turnips and potatoes Mandy tells us how she had spied some nibbles in her carrots and that was when she saw something 'very white' and 'very sweet' crunching away in the corner. I was thinking to myself, *Get on with it* a bit as by now I had guessed that this was a Lamb-Beth story. Mandy says there are lots of animals in this area so she wasn't entirely surprised to find an animal feeding off her 'produce' (posh word for vegetables) but when she saw Lamb-Beth's nametag she thought, *That's not a countryside lamb, that's a pet.* I could tell Mandy was posh and I didn't understand why she was doing all this hanging around outdoors business when she could be in a hotel lobby or something doing some serious complaining and drinking champagne like posh people are meant to spend their time.

'How did you find us, then?' Mum asks, hunching her shoulders to keep warm, crunching her boots through the leafy ground.

'Ah, now here's the best bit.' Mandy giggled. 'I

was on the phone to my daughter that evening – she is a journalist.'

'Like me,' I mouth.

'And I told her about the lamb with the nametag, in my patch, crunching away on some carrots. My daughter said she had been given a missing lamb poster by the sweetest little boy on a bike called Jamie . . .' WHAT?! I look to Mum and she looks to me but we don't say anything. Mandy continues, 'And this missing lamb had the same name! And here we are!' Jamie? JAMIE? JAMIE HADDOCK, WOW, just to think he used to be my enemy in school and now here is he saving my heart from breaking. How the tables turn! I feel glad. For a second I picture Jamie being my best friend instead of Will but it feels clunky and weird and I stop myself from getting carried away. Just because he's replacing me with Clementine doesn't mean I can replace him with anybody. That's not how friendship works. It's not a competition. Mandy slams her hands together, which breaks my trail of thought and leads us to a little wooden wagon. It is probably in the top ten most beautiful things I have ever seen ever.

'Wow, this is amazing.' Mum touches the side of the wagon, which is decorated in intricate beautiful flowers of gold and yellow and pink and blue.

'Thanks, I live in it!' Mandy beams. 'I couldn't even imagine living in a proper house now.' I thought this was *wonderful*. This really was a surprise for a posh person. A posh person *choosing* to live in a giant garden inside a wooden tent on wheels.

'It really is so fantastic.' Mum couldn't stop staring. I did like it but I was hoping Mum wasn't about to decide to move us into one of these. *I am not sharing a room with Poppy and Hector for anything*.

Mandy smiled, she has a big gap in the middle of her teeth big enough to slide a pencil into. 'It's a little tired now but it does the job for me and Sleep-Pig.'

'Who is Sleep-Pig?' I finally peeped out. The sound of my voice shocked even me as I hadn't spoken out loud in so long.

'This is she, the laziest, snooziest one of all . . .'

Mandy opens her wagon door proudly and there, under the amber glow of a little lantern, curled up on the most perfect, comfortable armchair, was a pale pink-haired pig, and wrapped up in its trotters was my Lamb-Beth.

'I never knew a lamb and a pig could get on so famously,' Mandy says, her eyes sparkling.

It really was the best feeling when Lamb-Beth saw Mum and me. She bounded up to our faces, licking us and kissing us and walking all over our laps and hopping and jumping and

tickling and bleating and being the cutest I had ever seen her. She wanted to introduce us to Sleep-Pig so much. Sleep-Pig was quite an old pig. She was slow and patient but affectionate and gentle. She sniffled our clothes and skin with her probing snout. Snuffling and huffing and inspecting every inch of us. She smelled like warmth and strawberries. Mandy was so excellent with her and rolled her over onto her back and tickled her tummy. This made Sleep-Pig grunt for approximately one hundred years and she got all happy and her whole mouth opened, showing us her chunky browning teeth.

Mum was laughing so much and kept squeezing my hand because the moment was so nice and Mandy was so friendly. When the evening started to drop down and the murmuring sky began to get shady, Mandy walked us back to our car with two boxes full of apples, turnips, carrots and potatoes from her allotment. It felt really special to have properly growed vegetables to eat. We stroked Sleep-Pig goodbye but Lamb-Beth seemed slightly reluctant to leave as she booted the earth with her little feet. Sleep-Pig snuffled her white springy coat and they stood there for a second as though they were gossiping.

'Can we keep in touch?' I pat Sleep-Pig and ask Mandy (even though I would have quite liked Sleep-Pig to answer but obviously she is a pig and that would be weird).

'It would be a pleasure. Let's send photographs of our little monsters to each other and please always feel welcome to come and visit now you know where to find us.' Mandy grins and we do too. I will never know how Lamb-Beth managed to make her way to this amazing allotment, but I am sort of glad she did.

Mum puts some chips in the oven and reheats some homemade vegetable chilli and when I hear Dad's key in the door I know the rest of our family is about to be reunited because Lamb-Beth is home. Poppy screams when she sees Lamb-Beth and hurtles towards her, knocking everything over. She scrunches

Lamb-Beth's face into a little ball and speaks to her in baby language, going, 'Oh, we missed you, we love you, love, love, love.' And loads of other nonsense. Throughout this experience, Hector is gently patting Lamb-Beth's back and combing her fur with his

gross jam-covered hand until he can no longer take the wait and completely knocks Poppy out the way so that he can have an air-robbing squeeze. Dad takes his time, but when the madness has died a little, he bends down with his cracking kneebows and softly strokes Lamb-Beth's face and ears, she snuggles into his hand and he laughs deep and all bear-ish. We are happy.

Grandma says there are a few answerphone messages for me and that Maggie's called loads, but Maggie isn't Will, is she? So it just doesn't matter and I don't bother or feel like speaking to Maggie at the moment. Now that Lamb-Beth is all 'safe and sound', as Grandma says, I just want to relax and paint my toenails every single colour of the rainbow, but all I can keep thinking about is all those wretched scarecrows at the allotment.

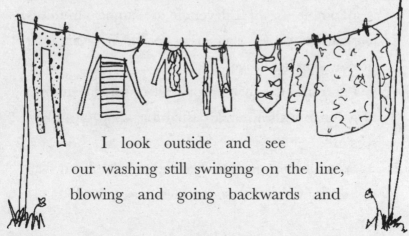

I look outside and see our washing still swinging on the line, blowing and going backwards and forwards, my dotty leggings, Poppy's swimming costume, Hector's rocketship pyjamas and Dad's curly wool jumper that he got from the very exact farm where we first met Lamb-Beth when she was just borned. The moon is slicing silver patterns all over the garden like knife shapes and then suddenly, as if by magic, Dad's jumper falls. Drops off the line, just like that. My heart stops and I panic for a moment.

That was weird. I want to run up to the kitchen window and get a closer look for myself, but I am very afraid, you see. What if a skeleton has grabbed his jumper to conceal himself underneath? Or what if a zombie uses it as leverage to clamber up to his feet and is slowly staggering to the door in long droopy slurring lunges?

I run into the living room but transform my run to a quick walk to look casual for when Grandma sees me.

'You all right, my love?' she nips and takes a swig of her red wine. 'You look as white as a sheet.'

'Speaking of sheets . . .' I start. 'The washing is still out in the garden.' Hoping she will come out and investigate and tell me it's a pile of nonsense.

'Oh, is it?' And as she uses all her might to pull herself up out of the sofa, her joints make tick-tocking noises like a xylophone made of bone and I think about all the washing she must have taken in over the years – probably even when she was young, in the olden days they had to wash clothes by, I don't know . . . dragging and beating rocks against them and leaving them to soak in the river, that would get tiresome.

Before I can stop and think the words tumble out. 'Don't worry, Grandma, I'll get the washing.'

'Darcy, do you know what you have made me? The happiest grandma in London.'

I go back to the kitchen, flicking my head over to the window to see the washing, and that is when I notice that *mysteriously* Dad's jumper is back on the line again and it is then that I have no choice but to open my mouth and scream.

SCARING-CROWS

Teddy was a tall person. Especially for a thirteen-year-old. He was so tall he could reach the precious posh glasses on the top shelf in the cupboard and put the angel on the Christmas tree without a chair to stand on.

Teddy lived in the attic room of a farmhouse and so as you can imagine his head was always completely decorated in bruises from where he had banged his head on the beams of the ceiling. He lived here with his miserable Aunt Beard and his aunt's out-of-control farm that Teddy absolutely hated. Teddy hated it here because Teddy was born in the city, where he liked the commotion and the wildness and the business. There was nothing he enjoyed more than peeling his eyes back as wide as they would go and soaking up the shops and the people and the bustling cafés and the honking

buses. He liked flowering his ears open as wide
as they could go and sponging up the arguments,
the bargaining, the worrying and laughter of the
city. But mostly Teddy loved it because it was
the life he knew with his mum and dad. It
was where he called *home*.

Teddy missed his parents desperately and
thought about them every day. There were
moments when he tried to remember what it was
like that morning, before they left. It
was his mum's birthday
and her and Teddy's
dad were going up,
up, up and away in
a hot-air balloon. He
remembered his mum's
long white dress and
oversized floppy
straw hat, her
hair blowing in
the spring air,

her cheeks flushed from excitement and his dad,
who hugged Teddy long and hard before he left,
smelling of musk and toothpaste. He couldn't
stop thinking about the air balloon, the way it
would hover and puzzle its way over the fields
and streets below, the way it would catch the
sunshine, the way it would meander over the
river.

And the worst that would happen would be
that the sunshine might bring out a freckly pink
on Dad's cheeks, maybe they would have a
bumpy landing, maybe Mum would lose her big
floppy straw hat to a gust of wind?

He never imagined they would never come
back.

Hope is a delicate emotion. It has to be
nurtured and taken care of, but after all it
is not truth, it is not real life. Eventually it
dissolves, evaporates in the hand like snow and
is gone.

After the funeral Teddy's Aunt Beard

adopted Teddy, she said she needed the extra help and hands of a strapping tall boy like Teddy to carry the pigswill and to drive the tractor. And so it was. Every morning Teddy was woken up to 2 snuffling pigs,

3 mooing cows,

4 clucking hens,

5 plucking ducks,

6 bleating goats,

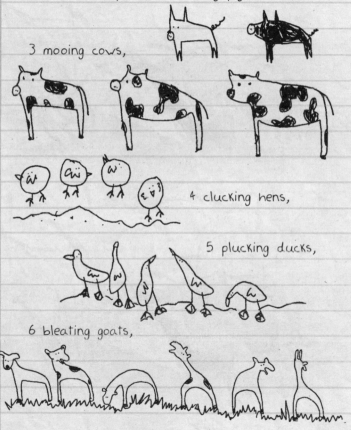

7 moaning sheep,

8 babbling sheep,

a horse named Sally,

a donkey named Geoff and a bullfrog that didn't actually belong to the farm but was always lurking about there.

'Darcy, bedtime!' Dad calls from the kitchen.

'Can I please just even have one more bit of time, please, to write this one bit down of my newest story?' Lamb-Beth leans her head onto my kneebow. I think she wants to know what is going to happen next.

'Five minutes!' Dad walks in and says, and then he does that thing when people pretend they've stolen your nose, which obviously isn't real but I quickly feel to find my nose anyway just to make sure. 'You better buy me a motorbike when you're a bestselling author!'

'Promise!'

I pick up my pen. It's really hard writing about a mean Aunt Beard when your own dad behaves pretty much like a king.

Aunt Beard was called Aunt Beard for the simplest reason that she was a bearded lady and she was wretched. She was a massive wreck of a woman with blustering big boobies

239

and she kept her hair in a long sharp fishtail
plait that was as spiky as the actual bones
of a fish. Her beard was also long and grew
into the shape of an upside-down mountain
and Teddy didn't like her one bit because she
was the grumpiest woman ever. She farted
massive explosive eruptions that smellled like
rotting guts and rancid sewage spinach mixed in
with nappies. She made fun of Teddy's name
and said it was a stupid name for a boy. She
never let Teddy have friends over, she never
let him ride his bike, she never let him make a
tiny mess from mud or paint or being alive. She
was always moaning and
groaning and shouting at the
TV and swearing, and
when she got out of her
bubble bath she never
washed away
the bubbles
down the

plug and she never ever *ever* let Teddy have
even a sip of her treasured Coca-Cola and
would often sit opposite him, gargling whilst he
drank his tap water.

But the main reason Teddy didn't like Aunt
Beard, on top of all those things, was that she
made scarecrows to go into the garden to protect
the plants and vegetables and she made the
scarecrows so scary that they should actually be
called Scare-*Everything-not-just-crows*.

They had huge horrible faces made out
of old potato sacks and straw hair and she
painted their faces in cheap make-up from the
chemist. But because Aunt Beard never wore

make-up herself she was very unpractised in this department, giving them big grizzly dripping unhappy bright red smiles and big gormless hollow deep eyes. She would dress them in old clothes from the charity shop: big woollen cardigans and shirts. She padded their bodies out with stuffed carrier bags so they looked really like humans and almost soft under all the clothes. It made Teddy feel embarrassed to complain about the scarecrows because Aunt Beard would call him a 'Big Girl's Blouse', but the few times Teddy did ask Aunt Beard to maybe not make the scarecrows *quite* so scary, Aunt Beard would tell him that the scarecrows had minds of their own and she had nothing to do with their creation. Teddy knew she was joking but it didn't stop them from being completely terrifying.

These thoughts and ideas would keep Teddy up in his bed all night worrying and losing his mind about how frightening and scary the scarecrows were, so much that he—

'This is the last call for Miss Darcy Burdock, the *last* call for a Miss Darcy Burdock, please evacuate the living area and make your way up to bed.' That was Dad pretending he was a pilot.

I didn't want to go, but I couldn't not appreciate his excellent attempts to get me up to bed.

That night I know I am so happy to have Lamb-Beth back as she is curled up at the end of the bed. I didn't ask her why or how she escaped and ended up at the allotment – for some reason that didn't seem important any more. She was home now. Poppy is here too because she also wanted to sleep with Lamb-Beth. Both of them are breathing so heavy in luxury sleep land; taking turns breathing so they sound like two kettles having an argument, but

I am not. I am hot and sweaty and unable to get to sleep.

I can't stop thinking about the scarecrows I saw at the allotment. It's funny how the things you don't care about in the day torture you mad in the night. I get up to reach my writing book and in the darkness, with the light off, I continue my story underneath the glow of my torch.

—often didn't sleep a wink at all. The thought of the scarecrows, lunging sloppily into his bedroom, bumping their straw-filled elbows against the door frame, heaving and heavy. He knew it was silly but he couldn't stop having these terrifying nightmares.

At breakfast one morning, over cereal, Aunt Beard stomped in and began being loud and taking up too much space and then she looked over to Teddy and grunted, 'You look tired, been out partying all night, have we?' She snuffled sarcastically into her coffee cup and stroked her beloved beard. This just angered Teddy even more.

'No. I am tired because I *couldn't* sleep because the scarecrows outside my window are *way* too scary and that gives me nightmares, I've told you this before.'

'Get over it and grow up,' Aunt Beard hissed as she swallowed her coffee. 'Look at you; you're hardly a baby. Unless you're a baby in a man's body!' She shook her head and left, snorting and sniggering to herself.

'Just because I'm tall doesn't mean I'm not a kid still! It doesn't mean I don't get frightened!' Teddy shouted after her. But it was no good. Aunt and her beard had left and only the cereal and milk heard his words.

If only his parents were alive, his dad

would never have stood for this. His mum would have punched Aunt Beard right on the nose. Teddy was no longer hungry and he took his bowl of leftover cereal and his tea and was on his way to the pigsty to give them the leftovers . . . when it hit him.

'Tall,' he said. 'I am . . . tall. I am . . . *tall.*' And something that his aunt had said about a baby trapped in a man's body . . . it suddenly triggered something. An idea, perhaps? An *escape*? And suddenly he had a terrifically good plan.

All day Teddy could not stop thinking about his idea: he thought about it whilst Aunt Beard guzzled her ice-cold Coca-Cola and stewed on it so long and so much he blew the idea up into little popping mind bubbles that he could almost

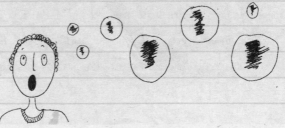

see drifting out of his head and into the air like cartoons that could burst.

And at dinner Teddy and Aunt Beard sat at opposite ends of the table, slurping the cold carrot soup and mung bean gratin that Aunt Beard had prepared and Teddy found himself unusually talkative, expressive, complimenting his aunt on every mouthful and every ingredient. He obviously didn't want to give the game away, but he just couldn't contain his excitement, and luckily she was ignoring him as usual so didn't get suspicious. And all the time he was thinking and planning and plotting and cooking up his wickedly excellent idea.

Ever wondered why when you are having a good time things rush by really quickly? And when you are having a bad time things ache and concrete themselves to the ground, not moving one bit.

Well, I know the answer to this and why this happens, it is exactly what was happening to Teddy at this moment in time. When you are having a good time you take off into a new magical happiness part of your mind and you forget about everything because nothing is more important than happiness. You forget about eating and drinking and listening and what everybody thinks of you and you forget about time. All that is important is the smile on your face, the butterflies in your tummy.

Then, unexpectedly Aunt Beard leaped up. Was it *that* time already?

'Right, time to put the animals to bed.'

This was Teddy's moment. He acted casual but really he was connecting the little idea dots in his head, hatching his perfectly formed plan.

It was dark outside, a spring evening, a light breeze fanning the boogying branches, scattering the leaves, wiggling like dangling earrings.

Aunt Beard was in the furthest pen from her house, putting the sheep to bed, when what was about to happen . . . happened.

She was just closing the gate on the pen, shutting in the moaning babbling sheep, when they all rushed to the corner of the pen, where they cowered, shaking and shivering.

'What's the matter?' Aunt Beard tried to be concerned but her instant reaction to absolutely everything was anger. 'It's not cold — why are you shivering like that?' And then she looked out into the night sky; nope, nothing. '*Weird stupid sheep*,' she muttered bitterly.

But as she turned to walk back towards the house . . .

Aargggghhhhh! I was beginning to scare myself! I wished Poppy would wake up but she was snoring like a whale. *Do whales snore?* Shut up, Darcy. You talk too much, you're thinking faster than what a rapper raps. If I were a rapper I'd call myself D Bizzle.

Something stood over Aunt Beard, towering over her, making her feel tinier and tinier and its face, its face was ugly and terrifying, maybe the most terrifying thing she'd ever seen. With the darkness slitting grey shards over its mortifying grimace she felt as though she had swallowed her own heart.

It was a scarecrow — one of *her* scarecrows, pacing, looming over her, shadowing over her, melting her into the ground. She stumbled back, fell into the pen with all the sheep, she was on her bottom now and the scarecrow followed her in, taking long, lazy drawn-out strides. Aunt Beard was on her back, scampering on the floor, her face as bleached as a posh packaged shirt. She had never felt such fear. When she was finally able to make use of her throat she screamed, she gasped, she shouted and then . . . she fainted.

Teddy took off his scarecrow mask and ran back into the house and even though it was a *bit* mean, he couldn't help but feel like jumping up and down and dancing and celebrating and so he did, and then he ran back into the house and straight to the kitchen where he almost ripped off the fridge door and took the first bottle of Coca-Cola he could find and unscrewed the lid before polishing off nearly the whole bottle in one mouthful. He burped and laughed his way up the stairs, took off his scarecrow costume and put his pyjamas on, getting into bed wearing a fabulous smile. Replaying the action like the best film he had ever seen, over and over and over. Of course his heart was racing from the excitement but he had to pretend to be asleep.

Moments later Aunt Beard, who had evidently now come round, came crashing into the house but she was screaming and sweating, searching for water, for a shot of whisky, for a cry, for a cuddle, for anything to make it easier to digest her traumatic experience. Teddy had to make the scene realistic so he began darting down the stairs, trying to hold the laughter in, asking what the fuss was about, pouring his broken aunt a cup of water, which she drank in one gulp. But always secretly smirking with satisfaction, keeping the fizzy happy Coca-Cola burps down. This was probably the best night of his life.

The next morning Teddy came down from an excellent night's sleep, stretching and yawning, only to find Aunt Beard sitting up stiff in her chair, a baseball bat on her lap, staring wide-eyed at the front door.

'I've got a job for you today, Teddy, seeing as

you're the *man* of the house and responsible: the scarecrows, they can come down. You were right, after all, I don't want you getting scared every night. I mean of course, I'd prefer to have the scarecrows up but you know, maybe until you grow up a bit, get a bit older, more mature, best to take them down?'

'Why can't you do it?' Teddy asked, innocently as possible.

'Oh, I would, I would, but I'm too busy and oh, I've got a bad back.' Aunt Beard pretended to lean over and massage her lower back, she was a shocking actress, the worst he had seen. 'But it should be done. Soon. Very soon, maybe even immediately, *now.*'

'OK,' Teddy giggled. 'OK. I'll do it now.'

And so he did.

I get up and find Grandma watching the TV, and by one look of our eyes to each other she opens up her arm like a wing and invites me in for a snuggle. It isn't long before I am sleeping as beautifully as violin music and the scarecrows are nothing but a faraway thought.

Chapter Sixteen

I wake up in my own bed but I don't remember getting there. I imagine a huge dinosaur rolling me carefully up onto his long neck and feeding me through my bedroom window, like a letter going into a letterbox, then stomping off to strip the trees of green stuff. Although in reality, Dad probably just carried me up the stairs and into bed. We don't much want to say goodbye to Grandma but Mum looks to me to be a bit 'grandma-ed' out so we cuddle her and I hold her rolls of chub in my hands and breathe in her rose petal smell. Grandma will probably have to be my new best friend because the Will Situation is not improved. I get Mum to write my sick note and she doesn't put much thought into it because I guess she can do what she likes, she's a mum after all.

Dear School Office
Darcy was ill so stayed at home.
Hope OK.
M. Burdock.

I am dreading school. My grey uniform isn't *as* itchy any more as when I first got it, which I guess is a positive, and at least my eyes aren't all stained red and Victorian horror maid any more now that Lamb-Beth's home. Dad takes us in today and we sing some of his punk songs in the car, which is actually quite a good way of releasing your anger and worries. I step out of the car and I can see Will, he is doing kick-ups with two other boys and laughing like an overly happy wretched hyena.

The sun is scaling the top of the school, making it look oddly fascinating in this light, like a pleasant important posh old building that you might see on a postcard or documentary. The heat is bringing all wonderful new colours of different shades, golden red and plush greens. Some birds peck at the crumbs of a cookie. I wave to Dad who winks back and I take a breath and go to walk past Will with his *friends*. I ready myself for us to have a fall-out of some kind. For him to be weird about things or make me feel even worse. But he dips his head, goes bright purple and ignores me, letting me walk past him completely without uttering a single word. I want to explode and everything to be over. I want to *do* school and then get home and into bed right away so I can cry my eyes out. I feel everything ending and rhyming with 'ad'. Sad, Mad and Bad but not Glad. Obviously.

I open up the heavy wooden door to take my sick note for my secretly *not* sick day off school. The receptionist signs it and ticks a few boxes, peering over me and back at her diary.

'How's your lamb?' she says, squiggling some words into a box.

'Fine, thanks.' I smile back but feel a bit confused. Nobody at school even knew I had a lamb, and *nobody* knew she was missing.

'So where did Lamb-Beth end up? How did you find her?' She tilts her head, completely interested in Lamb-Beth.

'Erm. How did you know Lamb-Beth went missing?' I ask, weirded out and mind-boggled.

'Oh, your thoughtful friend William was asking absolutely everybody – he handed out flyers and everything . . . just look at that wall over there . . .'

I was completely taken aback. In the entrance to the school was a whole wall with photographs of me and Lamb-Beth, Poppy, Hector, Mum and Dad all with her too, and one of Will, Lamb-Beth and me too, and underneath it read in giant letters:

PLEASE HELP ME AND MY
BEST FRIEND FIND LAMB-BETH

I stepped back a few places, nearly tripping on my rat-tail shoelace and shook my head in disbelief. I was so overly happy and smiling so hard my cheeks pushed up so they made my eyes blind. I ran outside and shouted Will's name over and over and over and ran towards him and he ran towards me, but pretended like he wasn't and when we reached each other we obviously didn't hug or anything, we just stood there, facing each other, panting and out of breath, until we both at the same time wheezed, 'Sorry.'

Chapter Seventeen

We enter the canteen together at lunch time and we see Clementine heading our way – so much had happened that I almost forgot about her. Missing Lamb-Beth made me forget completely about her ridiculous over-the-top birthday party at the posh restaurant . . . well sort-of-ish. She comes closer and I deliberately step back, lurking behind Will so she can accost him with her wretched self. But she just sneers at us and walks past.

'What's going on?' I gawp. 'Didn't you go to her birthday? Thought you two were *friends* these days.' The word friend feels oversized and ugly.

Will laughs. 'Ha! Not after I got injured in the football game. Apparently I was an *embarrassment*. She formally uninvited me to her birthday but I didn't care, I didn't want to go anyway. I think she only wanted to hang out with me so she could get to know all the older boys that played football. She's a selfish glory hunter. And yes, before you say it, wretched.'

I am deeply happy. Sometimes you need to let people find out that others are maggots themselves rather than showing them the way.

Lunch time is better than great because zillions of people keep coming over to me to tell me how much they enjoyed my story in the magazine and I feel proud and try to pretend I'm not interested or affected but inside I am mostly a fireworks display. Maggie, Gus and Arti pour over me and pat my back and squeal and say they had such great responses and that even the art teacher, who never even acknowledges them, took the time to say how much she enjoyed the 'hand-written organic feel' that my story had and that it felt very brave and artistic to publish it and that she can really feel the magazine taking an 'edgier' route.

Then Koala bowls over to me, all frumpy and thumpy with a grin as round as a basketball, and she kept calling me 'a mad genius' and offered me more space in the magazine to write creatively and even think about judging a creative writing competition! Me, being a judge? *Wow*. But then she got more serious and asks to speak to me *alone*. I nod, parting from Will, and follow her to a corner. I can see Olly on the other side of the canteen, throwing Wotsits into his mouth.

'Oh, great,' I sigh. 'There's Olly.'

'That's what I wanted to speak to you about . . .' she sprays at me. 'I heard you thought I didn't like your original story! That I thought it was weird . . . well, I do a bit, but I loved it, and when I spoke to you in the corridor that day, you seemed upset and I panicked, I wanted to say it was good – really good. It's been hard for me to say what I want because . . . I think Olly is a bit jealous of your writing and wanted me to put you down a bit about your hard work but I couldn't because you've worked so hard. The thing is . . .'

I bite my lip. *Where was this going?* I watch Olly, who is now watching us. He eats his Wotsits and then overly laughs at something that probably isn't funny, like he knows we're talking about him.

Koala continues, 'Ol and I have been friends for a long time.' *Ol?* Never imagined anybody to be on *Ol* terms with Olly. 'And, well, he asked me to be his girlfriend and I said YES!' Koala beams blissfully.

GROSS! YUCK! HORRIBLE! OUCH, PAIN

AND THUNDER IN MY EYES! NOOOOO-OOOOOOOOOOOOOOOOOOOOOOOOO! But I have to quickly win the control back over the muscles in my face and I smile and say, 'Oh, great,' through gritted teeth, and then I think about stupid Olly and everything he was saying to me about boys and girls not being able to be friends and remember that everybody has a motive and everybody can only relate their own thoughts and opinions to their own life. Nobody else's.

I watch Olly. He now looks different, it's like Koala had brought a certain shade of shine to his face. He waves and then looks away. Koala blows him a big ugly kiss and he 'air' catches it. GROSS. AARGH! PAIN AND ACID AND POISON IN MY EYES.

'Don't worry,' she whispers. 'I know he can be a toad.'

And I say, 'No! Don't be silly.' But I'm thinking, *Toadlette indeed.*

Olly waltzes over and, with hands on hips, drops

his head and says to me, 'Nice work on the story, Burdock, spot on, right in the kisser, yes.' And tozzles off, popping more Wotsits in his mouth, looking for others to harass, with Koala following behind.

'What was that about?' Will sniggers.

'I think that's called "eating your words",' Maggie replies, and oh she is right.

Will and I walk home together, catching up on so much. It turns out that it was Grandma who had called Will and the school to tell them to look for Lamb-Beth. I would normally be annoyed with her crafty ploy if it hadn't made us be back to best friends again. That display he made for me was the nicest thing anybody has ever done for me.

Mum is more than pleased to see me walk in with Will, but she doesn't mention anything or make it seem or feel weird. Instead, she just gives Will a squeeze and leads us into the kitchen where Poppy and Timothy are already munching and slurping on quesadillas (cheesy Mexican delicious things) and apple juice. Timothy and Will size each other up and introduce themselves, Will with a little flick of the eyes and Timothy with four air-kisses, *darling*.

'So ...' Mum smiles, sipping her coffee, 'can I finally *please* FINALLY read your story about the sisters in the magazine?'

'What story about the sisters?' Will interrupts; a long string of cheese joins his chin to his quesadilla.

'I changed it, I put a new story in,' I say to Mum in between chews, 'at the last minute.'

'How spontaneous, but I thought you spent ages on that other one?'

'Yeah, well ...'

'I hope you've got it written down somewhere. Go on then, let's have a look at what you've done.' Mum picks up the magazine, hugs her coffee close and opens the first page. 'It's in your handwriting!' she blasts in roaring excitement and then her eyes start at the very top.

The Invisible Link

For my friend, William Hopper

The earth cracked in two. One day. Just like that. Everybody naturally had to deal with the fallout. It splitted pretty much even. Like a halved orange or apple, the core on display like

268

the heart of a living breathing person in cry-sis.

It was sad because the earth had been a whole for so long. The roots of trees splitted and broked apart, the riva leaked and the fishes sprinkled out like confetti into the nothingness, the roads cracked and the pavements twisted, the houses felled apart brick by brick. The people were gripping onto the edge of the world, holding on, through the mania, to what was theirs. Some people's jobs were now on the other side of the earth, their friends and family, even their schools and favourite shops and *stuff*. Their whole entire lives.

And when it fell open and apart it sat, like the mouth of a Muppet, open and ajar, as though it was on a hinge and that was that. People had to start again. This was the way the world was now. This is what it had come to.

The distance apart meant that the world now felt like two separate planets a bit.

Completely. Naturally, people stuck to their own half now, their *bit*. And eventually over time, service resumed as normal, people got back to their worlds because they had to. Life goes on, as my grandma says.

The split affected everybody, of course, but you see the universe of stories is like a giant cake, and a story is but a slice of that cake. And the slice I want to cut is this one here, the story of a spider.

A young spider, who had just managed to strengthen her web to a soft strong cotton that sparkled under the glittery kiss of the sun and shone in the moody tones of the mighty milky moon. She had learned to travel, glide her web, to catch prey and to balance. To walk upside-down and point and pause and poise and position and prop and arch and angle. She was a fantastic, delightful and artistic spider.

She would web all day every day, working
fast to create her delicate embroidery of lace
that was her silvery almost invisible adventure
land that belonged to her — her architecture,
her world. And at night she would sleep in her
web, wrapped in a snug, silk warp of it all,
bundled in close but with enough room to spring
out if she needed. She was happy.

One day, whilst working, a tremor happened
that made her web wobble, causing the spider
to nearly tip off her stiches. She rarely wobbled,
she was more perfect than a tight-rope walker
and so she was anxious and frowned. It
was then she realized that the cracks in the
world were getting bigger, very slowly and over
time, but it was gently churning, breaking more
and more.

She looked at the hole in
her web and tended to it
immediately — holes in webs
are like holes in tights and will

only get bigger if not repaired. Just like holes in friendships too.

Across the way, on the other half of the world was another spider. A spider that saw his web-building as his livelihood, he was equally as talented: a solid spinner, a tipped delicate-footed, dangly, weave worker that could build just as rapidly. He built as gracefully and as elegantly as the spider on the other half of the world but had never spoken to her, had never even caught the reflection of one of her eyes in the light.

Until now.

'Are you OK?' he called.

'Who? Me?' she answered.

'Yes, you.'

'Why wouldn't I be?'

'The tremor, just then, I saw it knocked you off your web?'

'I'm fine, thank you!' she called back.

And so they carried on building and spinning and then just by magic, they had an idea. An idea so beautiful and strong, a life-changing, powerful idea. They both began to build a web towards each other. A bridge. Similar to the technique of sewing, they worked through and through, gossiping and nattering the entire time, getting to know each other; singing and humming, joking and debating, stitching and welding their glorious almost feathered yarn.

It was exhausting as the gap was very big and the spiders were so small; they worked through the day and night, catching flies and bugs for food, sleeping in mid-air and then starting again. Their web too was very thin so they had to go over the same patches many times to make sure the lines were strong and wind-secure. For months they built their bridge and they knew they were close to finishing when they looked up and saw no web left to build other than the loose end of either side of the bridge, waiting to be connected, to be tied up at last.

They lit up terrifically beautifully. They had done it and most importantly, what a wonderfully rich and remarkable way to weave the tapestry of friendship. They were friends, the very best of.

The following morning, the people of either half could not believe their eyes when they saw such a work of art joining their two worlds. They couldn't wait to visit either sides of these distant but now connected worlds; friends could reunite, celebrations happened and happiness was shared. Amazing how such a simple idea could change so much.

Both spiders were knighted for their efforts, were invited to a *proper* ceremony and then to the official opening and naming of the bridge, which they called *The Invisible Link*. Both spiders cut the ribbon to announce the opening of the walkway.

So much praise and celebration was happening for both spiders in their own halves of the world. They had interviews to go to, events to speak and spin at, workshops to lead, parades to host, dinners to attend that they almost seemed to be the only two to never actually even use the bridge that they had taken so long to build. They were so busy they just hadn't the time and after a while the bridge began to fray.

Everybody kept mentioning it, that the bridge had a few holes and repairs that needed tending to, and both spiders had meant to do it, but they just hadn't the time. People tried fixing it themselves but they weren't dainty enough to scuttle across, so they begged the spiders to go back and fix what they had started so the two halves of the worlds could continue as one. They began to all point the finger and blame each other and curse the other half for not protecting or maintaining their half of the world's bridge and they accused and argued and fought and raged so much that the last looping thread holding the bridge together fell apart.

The people cried for weeks. They were devastated.

It was awkward for the spiders; it sounds so simple and easy to do but it was a lot for them both to swallow. They had to admit, they had let their webbed bridge die - it was their fault and no one else's. They were too proud to begin building again, they were worried the other one wouldn't meet them at the other side, worried that the other wouldn't finish their side off or worse — wouldn't *want* to

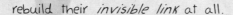

rebuild their *invisible link* at all.

So both spiders scuttled away and began
to build, but this time not to make a bridge
and make the world as one, but to separate.
Stubbornly, they began building a roof over their
half of the world that would contain each
half underneath it, with walls too, to separate
themselves even further, sheltering them from each
other, the sun and the wonder of life. It was
a dark and difficult time, building that was
painful for both spiders as it used a lot of
thread and took a lot of time and each stitch
was also hurtful and upsetting for the spiders
because neither really wanted to do this — they
were just being silly and proud and stubborn.
If only they could talk to each other and undo
the mess they had caused.

They built and built, webbing and making
until they had nearly finished and sat proudly
looking upon the two separate planets they had
created. Then, out of nowhere, they heard a

crack, a large cranking sound, a sucking sound, a churning sound and a pull . . . they had stitched so frantically hard on either side of the world and their waft was so strong they had stitched the world together again, without even realizing, making only a clean clear solid join.

The people couldn't believe it, those *clever* spiders with their tricks up their sleeves, nobody had seen this coming.

The world was as one. The spiders had unintentionally done it, but they had managed it all the same and so they, of course, being humble and graceful, bowed down to the praise and let the applause wash over them. They had secretly missed each other after all and sometimes . . . some things are just *meant* to be. Even when you try to escape them, they will just come to find you.

They celebrated for months on end and the spiders were awarded a tulip house to live inside, at the top of the world, together, exactly where they deserved, exactly how they felt.

The end.

Mum wipes the tears under her eyes away with her thumb and sighs all warbly, 'Funny how the tiniest of things can conquer the hugest.' Then she runs over to Will and me and hugs us really tight and says, 'Well done for getting through this Big School business, you two.'

And Will and I pretend to not want hugs loads but really I feel the skin of his hand against my hand and neither of us moves our hands but like not in a love way, obviously, we haven't lost our minds. I'm never ever going to call him William. Ever.

Poppy and Timothy snarl and snigger and pretend to be in deep conversation but really I know they are thinking . . . *Oh my God, is this what's to come?*

And I nod back at them as if to say . . . *Just you wait.*

Chapter Eighteen

Once I promised that I wouldn't make all the writing in my writing book about school and it feels like this is all I talk about now. That boring school and the boring people inside of it. Funny how we always make big grand statements in life and then scribble them out again with our actions. The rest of the next few months at school were fine. Nothing makes you realize how lucky you are more than losing the things around you that make you lucky in the first place. Like Lamb-Beth and Will. I feel like I've had a year that I'm never going to be able to forget. Every day I'm growing but I don't feel any older, that's the 'importance of a young heart', as my grandma always says.

On this point, nobody brings out the big kid in everybody like how Christmas does and it comes round faster than I could have even imagined. My mum and dad have been running around like lunatics all week, humming Christmas songs and eating and tickling us and hugging the Christmas tree like complete weird ones. It's the day before Christmas and I peel open the door with the '24' written on it – the last on the Advent calendar – and pop the silky milky chocolate in my mouth. D-E-L-I-C-I-O-U-S.

Next to it sits the 'home-made' Christmas card that the Pinchers sent to us. We've had it up there for weeks. It's a 'scene' by their fireplace (which we don't have, you have to be a posho if you have an actual real-life fire in your house, obvs). It's of John Pincher, sitting down on a fake log with a big cheery face holding a big sign saying 'HO, HO, HO!'

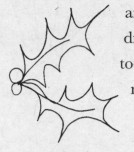

and then there's Marnie Pincher dressed as an (inappropriate, trying-to-be-sexy-ish) elf holding a bit of mistletoe and trying to kiss Santa (John Pincher) on the cheek and then the best bit of all is Donald looking so grumpy with reindeer ears on and a big fat red nose with reins tied to his back and he is looking likc hc absolutcly hatcs doing it so much and this absolutely makes my day. There is a bundle of presents all around them like a puddle of goodies, but I KNOW these will just be fake polystyrene or empty cardboard boxes wrapped in shiny paper because I went to the pantomime to watch Aladdin and shout 'HE'S BEHIND YOU!' loads and there was a massive big giant Christmas tree in the foyer and underneath were loads of presents and at first I couldn't believe my eyeballs so I made Hector go and tear the edge off one of the presents and he said it wasn't a present so I'm not a fool, you know.

Tomorrow is Christmas Day. Grandma is here

and has snowman ear-
rings on and is paint-
ing mine and Poppy's
nails red, gold and
green with a top layer of
sparkly glitter. We have
new pyjamas to wear
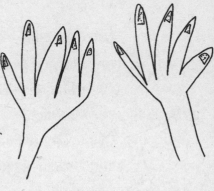
for tonight, which are all ironed and on our beds,
and matching stockings waiting at our headboards.

We sent our letters
off to Santa
AGES ago so
he better not try
and lie and say
he didn't get
them or else I
will be furious

Angrosaurus rex absolutely instantly immediately.
The shopping has been done so the fridge won't
shut, even when Dad slams his whole entire body
against it. But I peep in and all I see is floor to roof

of fridge space jammed with delicious things that I want to eat every second except for all them sheets of ghastly wretched smoked salmon taking up all that space so it means the turkey has to lie floating in the bath, like a turkey on holiday, in Turkey.

I see some scrummy apple and mango juice at the back and badly want a sip (we never usually have juice other than squash so I'm obviously a new degree of overexcited about this) and I reach for it and a million things pour out from the shelves in the fridge and tip onto the floor and a tub of cream drops and straight away splodges onto the floor and I try to clean it, but Lamb-Beth immediately takes this

as a cue to start licking up every drop like the animals do in Disney films that lick the plates all clean like in *Snow White* and stuff. It's so unhygienic and horrid and Dad comes in before she's managed to lick it all up and says, 'No, she will get sick,' and picks her up and pulls her away. 'Cream's too rich for her,' he says to me and I'm thinking, *Lamb-Beth's not a spoiled SNOB if that's what you're meaning by too rich.* He's cross now because the fridge has started to make that whinging noise it does when it's been open for too long and it's proving to be really very tough to puzzle all the food back in and he is getting crosser and crosserer and more red and more annoyed, plus he's got all specks of glitter in his beard from all the cards and sparkly baubles and it's making him all itchy and miserable because everything is everywhere.

And finally he says, 'No going in the fridge without asking. It causes an avalanche.' And I say *OK*. And think about all the other treats inside the fridge and I feel exactly so much like Aladdin at the pantomime and how he wanted to badly get inside the cave to get to the treasure. Still, at least crisps don't live in the fridge.

I insist on only listening to extra-cheesy wheezy

Christmassy music blaring at volcanic volume out of every speaker in the house and so that's what's happening, of course, because nobody can tell you off for having happy cheery spirit and Poppy is dancing with Lamb-Beth who obviously has reindeer horns on but looks way better than stupid dumpy dumb Donald does on that Christmas card.

The door knocks and it's . . . the Pinchers. *Sigh*. Speak of the devil (as Grandma would say even though I don't know what that means).

'*MERRY CHRISTMAS!*' Marnie wails. I say *wails*, I mean *screams*, and totters in wearing stupid too-high-for-real-life heels. She is dressed in that same gross sexy-ish elf outfit with fishnet tights. Her eyes are all red and drowsy like she's been sipping on the old whisky. She has lipstick on her teeth.

Donald tramples in right after her, playing his handheld

287

PlayStation business without lifting his head up even once, not even to say hello, which if I'm lucky will result in a good old trip-up and teeth-smashing-out experience. And then John stands at the door, leans back, all proud and pleased, props a Santa hat on his head and with a big bin bag of presents in his grip roars, 'HO! HO! HO!'

We got some quite good presents from the Pinchers. Dad and Hector both got remote-control helicopters which light up, which Dad seems to be more into than Hector. Hector's mostly interested in the box that it came in. Mum got what Marnie calls 'smellies' which means all stuff for the bath and annoying candles and soap and stuff but I think the word 'smellies' makes it sound like it is a basket of potions or a heap of smelly socks and is quite misleading. Marnie says, 'Can never have too many smellies, can you, Mollie?' to Mum way too many times, and I can tell it's annoying Mum same as me because you obviously could have too many. You can have too much of anything . . . except chips probably.

Lamb-Beth gets these chocolate buttons that are even safe for animals to eat and we all try one and it's OK and smells chocolaty but tastes not sugary one bit. I can see them coming in useful in case of emergency (i.e. the biscuit tin being all emptied out). Poppy got a karaoke DVD and microphone which is really pretty siiiiiiiiicccccckkkk and I'll really look forward to that later when nobody is around, and I get this really cool bead necklace and bracelet kit that means I can make my own jewellery. I'm already one step ahead and think I could really just start a quite profitable business – make the jewellery – sell it – complete excellent profit basically. They even got Grandma some expensive fudge, but to be honest that's insensitive if you ask me because her teeth might fall out so it's probably best if I eat it.

After burning my mouth on loads of Mum's home-made sausage rolls and devouring so much chocolate that there are tiny coloured wrappers all on the floor like little bits of chopped-up stained-glass window, we all watch a bit of TV and I look through the planner and it's really fun because all the best films are on that remind you of being smallerer and ones that Hector hasn't seen yet that I can't wait to show him, and Donald is doing a really good job of not saying 'this is *so* dumb' or 'how babyish' at everything. When they leave we say goodnight and Marnie falls over on the doorstep and scratches her kneebows a bit, but laughs it off probably because it's Christmas tomorrow. We wave goodbye to them and close the door.

'Phew, right, that's that then.' Mum flops onto the sofa and then Dad sits next to her and says something containing a big swear word which obviously

I'm not allowed to write here but basically means 'I'm glad they are gone'. Mixed with relief.

Dad puts Hector on his shoulders and I get on his back and Poppy leaps on his feets and holds his hands and we walk to the kitchen like a crazy wobbly new zombie hunchback creature-zoid we have created. Dad plays up to it, groaning and moaning and making gravelly husky noises with his throat and murmuring and he slumps up to Mum and says, 'What a pretty lady.' And she screams and laughs and then says, 'OK, enough now, Mary Berry's on TV' (who is this gentle baker lady), so Dad takes us into the kitchen, still being a zombie monster, and we are all laughing but Hector is *screeching* at a high enormous pitch because it's his *thing*. And then Dad peels us off like PVA when it gets stuck to your hands and sits us on the counter.

'Right, kids,' he announces, 'we have to leave out Santa's goodies so he has something to eat when he drops the presents off.'

'Not without me!' Mum shouts from the other

room and then runs in like a small child, carrying Lamb-Beth in her arms, wiggling her bum and waggling her tongue. Mum is still such an excellent child.

We leave out eight carrots for the reindeers that Dad says we don't have to peel because the deer like the skin, a mince pie for Santa and a glass of milk and a can of beer. It's all just too exciting that it's Christmas the next day so we all want to go to sleep as quickly as can be. So Hector, Poppy and I run upstairs, brush our teeth, wee and get into our new pyjamas and lie in our rooms – blinking and crinkling our eyes pretend shut but we're too excited and so I run round to Poppy's room, peeping my head round the door only to find her head peeping round her own door waiting for me to come. After a big bit of giggling we then decide to drag my mattress into Poppy's room which is loads of effort plus more because we have a laughing fit the whole time and Dad tells us to be quiet and then Mum says that we are a hassle and: 'Father Christmas won't like this very much.'

And then by accident I tell Mum to *GO AWAY* and I'm in trouble and Dad takes me downstairs and gives me a pointy finger chat that makes tears bubble in my eyes like deep wells for a second but then we cuddle and it's OK-ish and Christmas is nearly on the edge of being 'cancelled', I think, but when I get back upstairs Mum has helped Poppy put my mattress on the floor and so Hector and Lamb-Beth sleep there and Poppy and I sleep head to toe in her bed.

I say sorry and even the *love* word to Mum and she says it's all right and she understands. For ages Poppy and I keep kicking each other and being sweaty and laughing and try to go 'OK, let's sleep now, goodnight' and be silent for one moment before bursting out into laughter again and in the end it's Hector that screams 'GO TO SLEEP!' which is a first for him and we are a bit stunned but it works.

We wake up at 5 a.m. Too early to even be alive and once we're awake it's just too hard to go back to sleep because the Christmas feeling just hangs in the air like twinkly LAAAAAAAAAAA.

I listen to hear if Grandma has woked up as she obviously wakes up at zero o'clock but she was up late last night and I can't hear her, and Mum especially warned me NOT to wake ANYBODY up under ANY ENTIRE circumstance. We are struggling to think of what to do – we can't get up yet because it's way too early and we will get into trouble and they will be in a bad mood and no amount of coffee and smoked salmon will solve that.

So Hector pulls out his dinosaur sticker book and we do that for a bit. I absolutely love dinosaurs and this book, because it tells you exactly how to say each dinosaur's name in broken down bits, for example Tyrannosaurus rex will say TIE-RAN-NO-SAW-RUS-REX so you can say it like a true expert. We start to get hungry and our bellies are rippling and rumbling and grumpyling like huge moody beasts that need feeding, but after being told off for spilling the cream and ruining the fridge layout I just know we are not allowed.

'But we're sooooooooooooooooo hungry,' Poppy moans, rubbing her tummy. 'Can't we just mouse-step down and get a few bits and bobs?'

'Or even a glass of tap juice?' Hector adds; his eyes look desperate and dehydrated like he could do with a few more blinks.

We *probably* could, but I just know Mum and Dad don't trust us to not go into the living room before they wake up in case we sneak-peep at our presents, plus I got in trouble before bed too and Christmas could still maybe even get cancelled.

I take out my writing book and write in massive letters:

BANG. WALLOP. PLOP. POOF. PUFF.
GLONG. BONG.

And then, big enough for everybody to see, the word:

OUCH.

'What you doing?' Poppy asks, and climbs off her bed and into our mattress floor bed. I was feeling a bit inspired by the fairy wings hanging off the back of Poppy's door.

'I need a name, a name for a girl fairy – who can think of one?' I ask.

'KARATE!' Hector shouts.

'OK, good. I like it, Karate.' I smile and write KARATE down. Poppy looks upsetted. 'What's wrong?'

'I want her to be called Petal.'

'NO!' Hector protests. 'That's an ugly name.'

I let them squabble whilst I wrote, then began to read the beginnings of a special Christmas story:

'Karate-Petal had fallen out of her tree house. She was not supposed to be falling out of anything, let alone the tree house. Especially not in the daytime. She had broken the fairy rules. *Big time*. Which wasn't surprising as she was pretty much the most naughtiest fairy of all time. She dusted down her mucky murky grey skirt which, for a fairy of any kind, was fairly dirty, but for a newly sparkled indoor fairy was an absolute no-go. Nah-ah, nah, darling, negative.'

'I love it!' Poppy says.

'Can she maybe broked a wing?' Hector asks. *Good idea.*

'And when she stood, *ouch,* she realized she had broked a wing. Its glassy hinge collapsed and tilted to the left, like a bent-back kite swaying in the breeze and the net was torn and frayed. She scrunched her face up, used her core strength and tried to buzz herself up to a height, except the great force of the smashed wing just allowed her to bump along at an angle, like she was sleepy or drunk.'

'And there was blood everywhere!' Hector cooks up, his eyebrows wriggle.

'Yuck! Hector, it's Christmas Day. You horrible.' Poppy pokes her tongue out.

'OK, a little bit of blood, but it's all right because

fairy blood is . . . wait for it, Poppy . . . sparkly like our nail varnish!' I say and carry on writing. Poppy nods in approval.

'Karate-Petal looked up to her tree house, at its dizzy height and tried first of all to use the weeds and twigs to begin scrambling up the tree to safety, but she was useless at climbing as she hadn't yet had her outdoor induction day. She hit the ground with a frustrated bump. She tried calling up, shouting the many names of her brothers and sisters, but her voice was as tiny as the sound of an apple growing. Her curiosity had got the better of her for the last time.

'Then what happens?' I ask them both.

They stare at me blankly.

'What can happen?' Poppy asks, terrified of the pressure.

'Anything.' I nod. 'That's why I write because you can make *anything* happen.'

Poppy sucks on the thought like a boiled sweetie.

'A monster comes!' Hector growls, his eyes popping out of his head.

'Good!' I announce and write some more, reading it out as I write it down.

'Karate-Petal began to cry until she heard its unmistakable stomps, its churning, furious, roary, gritty, growly noise.

'What shall we call the monster?' I ask.

'Ummm . . . Ripper . . . no . . . Roarer . . . no . . . Ruiner . . . no . . .' Hector is really *into* this. His brain is a practical joke.

'The Ripper-Roarer-Ruiner-Beast!' I whisper-shout and write it down: 'The scariest most vicious creature that roared the land. Karate-Petal panicked and yelped her tiny head off, trying now much more frantically to scamper back up the tree to safety but she couldn't and the Ripper-Roarer-Ruiner-Beast was coming closer and slobbering and its sharp yellow eyes were squinting and its teeth were sharp and its claws were thick and pointy and in one swoop it swallowed Karate-Petal.'

'NO!' Poppy screams. 'Why?'

'Wait!' I whisper, trying to bring her voice down so she doesn't wake Mum and Dad. I continue . . . 'But he didn't *eat* Karate-Petal. He carried her in his mouth through to the kitchen where he lived. He was a family dog and his name was actually Cookie and he was harmless, but of course the fairies only knew of him as the scary Ripper-Roarer-Ruiner-Beast that dug up the garden and ripped up the rubbish bags and weed all over the place. They were tincy and tiny and helpless compared to him.'

Poppy strokes Lamb-Beth, happier with how the story was going. I start again.

'And then Cookie fell to sleep. Of course Karate-Petal was still terrified. She couldn't believe her heart was still beating and the inside of the Ripper's mouth was *disgusting*. BIG yellow teeth and a FAT red tongue and his breath STANK of meat and dirt and poo. But she was grateful; covered in slobber, but still grateful to be alive. She tiptoed down the tongue, carefully holding her broken wing close so it didn't scratch his cheek and wake up the beast. And then she opened up his jaw with all her might, like the boot of a car, and broke free. *Where was she? What was she to do?*'

'I know! I know!' Poppy shouts. 'She sees the giantest most best Igloo Palace, but really it's just the fridge, fulled of all foods like our one at Christmas and Karate-Petal has been told about all the wonderfullest things inside and has seen drawings and pictures of it in her tree house and she wants to get inside!'

I give Poppy my pen. She looks surprised and stunned.

'Write it down,' I say.

'I can't. I don't know how to spell.' She bites her lip.

'Me neither.' I shrug.

'Yes you do, you're always writing.'

'Doesn't mean I can spell,' I reassure her.

'But I'm not even good.'

'Can you talk?' I ask.

Poppy nods and crinkles her nose a bit.

'Then you can write.' I smile.

'But my handwriting isn't even neaterer.'

'Look at mine.' I show Poppy all the pages and pages of my writing book, sprawling in inky mess, like a spider that has found itself drowning in a pot of ink and has helplessly clawed across the page in preserving agony to get to safety mixed in with a waiter from the Chinese restaurant.

'Are you sure?' she says and holds the pen.

'One hundred per cent sure.'

Poppy writes and then hands the book back to me: her handwriting is *so* much neater than mine. Don't know what all the fuss was about, to be honest. I carry on.

'But how to get up? Her wing was broked and she wasn't good at climbing – she had just found that out. She needed to think of something. She tried jumping and sliding and shimmying but the walls of the Igloo Palace were so shiny she just kept sliding back down again and hitting the ground with a bump. This was horrible and pathetic and she was tired and homesick and everything was so *wrong*. And she began to cry. Little tiny fairy sniffles.'

'Oh, poor Karate-Petal,' Poppy sniffed.

'I know, I know . . .' Hector cries. I give Hector the pen to write what happens next and he is completely confident and has no trouble writing exactly what he wants to say. I think he thinks his writing makes sense, but luckily for us he speaks every word out loud because mostly his words look like flattened Frisbees and we would have zero idea what he was on about. This is what he says out loud:

'BBBBBBBBBBBBZZZZZZZZZZZZZZZZZ. BUZZZZ. BUZZZZ. Karate-Petal looks up to see a huge fly flying all around the window. And they were friends and then the fly takes Karate-Petal up onto the top of his body because Karate-Petal has even a poorly sawed and broked wing but it's OK because they zoooom up over to the fridge – yeah, Igloo Palace.'

Poppy starts, 'Yes, and the fly spoke in lots of ZZZZZZZZ's.'

'Yeah, that's good,' I zay. (See what I did there, I put a Z instead of an S for fly language.) I took the pen.

'They waited until a human opened the door to the Igloo Palace and then they would leap in and visit this magical incredible land.

'They waited.

'And waited.

'And waited.

'Meanwhile, the fairies in the tree house had noticed that Karate-Petal was missing and they were deva-stated and so worried and couldn't find her anywhere.'

'We know how it feels to have something you love losted as well, don't we, Darcy?' Hector asks, and yes, he is talking about Lamb-Beth, and that means yes, we do know how that feels. The worst.

Poppy steals the pen from my hands, not meanly, more over-excited. 'They searched everywhere and when Cobweb, Karate-Petal's little sister, poked her nose out of the tree-house window, she saw the great door to the Igloo Palace open and her big sister fly inside. "SHE'S IN! SHE'S IN THE IGLOO PALACE!" she cried, and everybody panicked –

they all knew they had to ride Cookie and to get him to take them to the Igloo Palace, which was fulled to the brim with such most delicious Christmas treats. And they were not never even scared of the dog any more. OK, Darcy?'

'Good, Pops, well done, OK, they are not scared any more.'

Hector takes the pen back off Poppy and this annoys her and she goes to hit him but I say, 'It's Christmas, don't fight.'

So Poppy fake smiles at him and Hector then decides to give the pen to me and says, 'Can you write, they knowed Cookie is not a monster but a doggie now and he collects them and they all get inside and all the fairies have a most wonderful party with all the food?' I write it and he smiles, Poppy rolls her eyes but Hector looks proud. He then takes the pen himself and writes:

'The end.'

'That's not the *end*.' Poppy scrunches her face up.

'Oh, sorry. I forgotted. All the flies all come in too

and ruin the fun time,' Hector giggles.

'No!' Poppy screams. 'No flies, just fairies.'

'Fairies are for girls,' Hector spits.

'Flies are for boys,' Poppy says through gritted teeth.

'Fairies *and* flies are for both girls and boys, they are for everyone,' I say, and both Poppy and Hector mumble, 'See? See?' under their breaths.

'Now why isn't the story finished?' I ask Poppy.

'Because I wanted to write about them eating the food inside the Igloo Palace,' she says.

'Well, why don't we eat it now ourselves and write about it later?'

We agree on that one because the clock says 6.35 a.m.

It's a bit of a rushed story, but it's OK, we've passed the time and we're nearly allowed to wake up Mum and Dad and be starting Christmas.

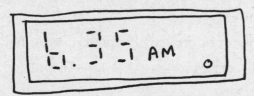

Having a whole lovely day with so much to look forward to, the end of another year and the beginning of a new one. We all stand up, with a juddery feeling in our tummies. So much has changed, so much is about to. What a life.

I put my hand on the doorknob and open it . . .

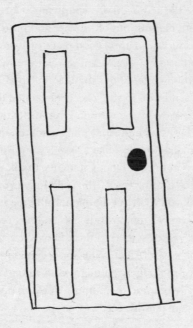

Acknowledgements

Thank you to my agents Cathryn Summerhayes and Becky Thomas. Becky, Darcy still belongs to you.

Thank you to WME in the UK and US offices, especially to Siobhan O'Neill, Katy Brace and Laura Bonner.

Everybody at the Random Towers: my editor Lauren Buckland who knows Darcy better than me some days, thank you for your wisdom, energy, playfulness, bravery and support. You are brilliant. Andrea Macdonald, for your wonderful ideas and, well, you made me an octopus out of crochet and posted it to my house – so obviously you are a good piece of work. My publicists, Lauren Bennett and Harriet Venn, who have now visited nearly all the train station coffee shops the UK has to offer with me in the last year. Thank you for the excellent excited flurry you form for me, you take care of me so well. Lauren Bennett - thanks for pushing boundaries with me and making all things impossible possible (like making me feel like I have a stunt double so I can be at two places at once!). Dom Clements: thank you, you have yet again created a thing out of the stuff I give you. You are so creative. Thank you to Annie Eaton and Philippa Dickinson for letting me get Darcy's mum drunk quite a lot. I really appreciate that. You never put iron fences around my writing and I am grateful. Thank you to Alex Taylor for organizing me short-notice taxis – I just really need them. Charlotte Portman for all of your hard work and the yummy steak, thank you. All of Random House makes me feel very supported and taken care of.

Thank you to Sue Cook for the copy edit, I know it must be difficult agreeing to all that 'worserest' spelling.

Thank you to all at Booktrust for your support and encouragement.

Thank you to the special glittery teachers, librarians, bloggers, journalists, photographers, promoters, booksellers that LET me DO this.

Thank you to all the generous and supportive writers I've met.

Thank you to my old audience and thank you to my new one. You are all mad.

Thank you to Dhillon Shukla for his photography.

Thank you to my friends who have read the work, come to the readings with hundreds of kids at 11 a.m. with hangovers, let me ramble on in my 'method-writing voice of a ten-year-old'. I love you.

Special thanks to Bobby Mac for pretending to be a child so I could try out all my ideas on his brain.

And thank you to Ricky Briggs for being the loyal staff and for driving me to loads of places that are far away.

. . . That's a lot of thank yous but it's so special to have your name in a book and this lot all deserve it! If you know me at all, you will understand this is true.

To my beautiful, colourful, enriching and INSPIRING family, thank you. I am OBSESSED with you, but you know that and it's getting boring how much I love you (that's a lie, it never gets boring.)

Daniel. You are blatantly the king of the palace in my head; the throne is yours and will always belong to you. I am a maniac. X